THE ENDLESS PINES

Jeffrey Koval Jr.

To friends and family, past, present, and future.

the endless pines

In the mid-1980s, there were a series of seasonal storms that you will not find adequately covered in the usual archival format or in weather databases, specifically those built to chronicle the regions making up the blindspots of national research laboratories. Though New Jersey had quality atmospheric-research coverage by labs in both Philadelphia and at the Sandy Hook Marina (as well as multiple smaller hubs throughout the region), during this period there were issues concerning jurisdiction and legal reviews of the laboratories' work and ongoing operation contingencies.

Combined with multiple agency-level labor strikes throughout both the local and national levels, there were historic failures of data-capture and severe weather reporting. Nevertheless, life went on. The people who lived in these so-called blindspots had existed before the government had hovered their magnifying glasses over the unique ecosystem that made up the southern portion of the state, the region known as the Pine Barrens, and they would presumably continue to exist long after any studies exhausted their funding.

Attempting to navigate this hectic climate as unnoticeably as possible, an aspiring utility worker named Peter Demetri spends a summer in these woods, taking a series of odd-contract-jobs under the table, attempting to build a career and traverse safely through the endless pines.

ONE

This is your Professor Emeritus to Be, young Joel Emerson, and you're tuned into Your Local, the Eagle 1280 AM. As you all know, we have big things in store for the station, having been blessed with oh-how-fortuitous of a spring, a true season of spiritual growth and cleansing. Who knew that the big guys and the fat cats with bursting wallets could actually do something for us, the little guys, and actually spread the wealth a little. A government working for the people, what a concept! How novel!

In case you haven't been in the loop or are just listening in for the first time since you and the other snowbirds came back home from sunny Florida, the limited staff we keep here at the Eagle, myself included, have been tirelessly working away at obtaining the prerequisites for a handful of national grants doled out from Washington. How's Orlando! That's right, our sleepy little station has a chance to put on its big boy pants. Preliminary work has already started, they've broken ground in my own backyard near the State's best kept secret, Stockton College. This time next year, we very well may have our own top of the line service running from Galloway through Mount Holly to Burlington City, hooking us up into the Philly suburbs and America beyond! Imagine me, your beloved professor, in syndication! What fresh hell! How exciting!

Well, that's what the suits tell me at least. I'll let you in on a little secret. I'm looking out the window right now (overcast day in the Pines, not much precipitation, but low burn advisory, good stuff!) and though I'm not, were I a gambling man, I'd be down in AC right now, putting down my tenureship and two-months-mortgage on this little endeavor not being completed for... let's say four years, keep it nice and even. But I'll still be here. Heck, by then I won't be "To Be" and might even be on your airways full-time. How's that, Dean! Pluck one thorn from Stockton's backside and place it firmly into that of society's!

Ah, we have fun here, gang. Don't forget that. Coming up on the hour are our Golden Oldies. Beyond that, who knows. I'm thinking we fire up the chakras and blow open some Third Eyes at the ten am hour. I have plenty of articles I wish to share with you from some friends and colleagues out West. But first. . .

Pete Demetri stepped on the truck's brake and turned the key. The vibration of the heavy work truck sputtered to an abrupt silence and he was immediately reminded of how late in the season it was. The air condition now gone, the cab almost immediately began to feel suffocating as it warmed up to the natural temperature outside, a balmy mid-80s in the last week of May. Jersey summers could creep up on you, but once they had set the tone for the year, you'd usually be able to gauge how long it would be until you no longer felt permanently sticky with the season's humidity. Today's guess meant that it wouldn't be until at least September or October that the mild temperatures would return. Mild weather. That ship had sailed about two weeks ago and Pete sighed as moved in his seat, the denim jeans and flannel overshirt seeming horrendously out of place. He still liked working outside, but could never find the outfit appropriate until that fabled, far-away autumn finally arrived. Even then, he would end the day matted in sweat. He knew a guy who owned only two sets of work clothes and didn't know how the dude didn't constantly reek of body odor. Maybe that was something he would eventually learn the mastery of, if and when he ever made it into an actual apprenticeship route, rather than… whatever this current set-up was.

The truck could have probably been left running. It was hot enough outside to warrant a few more minutes of peace. Pete reached under the vacant passenger seat for the memo pad and flipped to the next clean page. He quickly wrote some meaningless details from the day, if only to document to himself that he had put in the hours. Before he began the practice of note-taking and making a rough project log, Pete realized that days of his own life had begun blurring together. It was not anything too alarming, you know, not worthy talking to a doctor about or anything,, but the recognition of the fact did concern him to a point. His career had really only just begun. If he looked back in ten years, how much of his waking life could he be expected to remember if he did not have some piece of tangible recollection, some sort of record? Thus, the memo pad became his silent best friend. One of the only actual friends he had, in fact. Now that was another observation that had given him enough concern in recent years. But it, too, was one relegated as something to keep an eye on and take care of, eventually. Maybe. He had been keenly aware of the grant programs the erratic radio host had touched upon, about the work to be done around and for the small radio station in the Pine Barrens, but it was interesting to hear someone else reference something he was loosely involved in, out in the wild.

He was not yet full union or a part of any trade school, so poor Pete here only had the luxury of per diem day labor to look forward to. For better or worse, and self-directed derision had always leaned it firmly towards the latter, he was a scab. Finding work had only recently been a winning game what with all of the labor strikes and controversy that had been brewing over. Federal and state governments were hemming and hawing about natural disaster responses and, locally, there had been a lot of finger pointing over who or what authority was actually responsible for cleaning up whenever God had decided to throw a wrench into the "smooth sailing" (Pete snorted to himself) that was life in southern New Jersey. A Federal agency had been ramshackled together a year or two before Pete got into the game (that is, needed to work after graduating high school without much of a plan, but was too late along to ever think of finding a skill to do with his hands) and called itself FEMA. Trying to run things efficiently was a case study in disasters itself, but Pete had never thought he would have to deal with it in any personal or professional capacity. He was, of course, wrong as the utility workers unions, both local and national, had become fed up with the ticker tape parade of the red variety and an unignorable deficit in timely payments. So, now that some disaster mitigation had to be started, whether on our roads or in our forests, and the people who actually knew what they were doing were standing up for themselves and on a series of strikes, that's where Pete and his small band of coworkers came in.

His boss was actually a small business guy, they called him Mr. Z. The little Italian dude was a plumber by trade, but was attempting to pivot to assume more of an advisory role in his later years. That didn't stop him from still showing up to routine jobs and weekend morning estimates in his sweats and a jacket, glasses falling off his face and dropping his utility belt whenever he became bored of holding it up any longer. It was kind of amusing dealing with the man, because he was clever as fuck and knew his stuff, but he was constantly warring with and going on about lifelong friends he had in the union after his spectacular exit just before his "official" retirement.

Pete never delved too deeply, he only knew the guy for a few months at this point, but the gist he got was that there was some bad blood about Mr. Z's expulsion from a particular trade group after it came to light that he had had some colorful investments in Atlantic City that conflicted with multiple shops' contracts. Throw a rock and you were bound to hit someone legally, or at the very least, ethically, unclean in South Jersey. Mr. Z was just a funny example of such. Some were criminal and others were just characters, but there was a certain scent that was unmistakable and impossible to ignore for anyone who wasn't perpetually doused in the stuff, for anyone who was not so *fortunate* as to have spent an entire life or career in some of the particularly charming backwaters in the state's legal blindspots.

Either way, either as a way of getting back at the people that he felt had snubbed him after a lifetime of service, or whether he was just trying to earnestly run a business and send his grandkids to college, Mr. Z's contracting services were still available, and Pete was one of the newer lackeys he employed to get boots on the ground and have said ground broken through a period of work delays, change orders, and all the other fun stuff and pleasantries that had made contracting disaster relief a living hell.

Now, Pete wanted to be like his late father who was an electrician. Worked for years alongside civil engineers and an alphabet soup of government agencies towards the end of his run. Always firmly civilian himself, but within proximity of enough nexuses of lucrative contracts and job security that he instilled the idea that this was a secure means of employment to pursue to his son. There were plenty of options. Maybe follow a lineman's route, there were a few counties down here that he knew he could apply to whenever things cooled down. But who knew when that would be? He realized that there was an odd mentality in play as a hired hand for disaster response and reconstruction efforts. There were things about your own community and towns that you had never wanted to see in the newspapers. Fires, floods, the like. But when that was your bread and butter and would result in your income and financial security… well, it was an odd headspace to dwell in. Like a kid wanting a snow day, but as an adult with ulterior motives and bills to pay. The more disastrous a streak of misfortune could be, the more hours he could put in for Mr. Z's shop. The more money he had saved away, the easier it would be to breathe when the time came for him to become a student, an apprentice, once again.

As the truck continued to tick and cool down, inversely becoming more warm and uncomfortable to sit in, Pete thought about the months ahead and about his "snow day" comparison. It was just about to be hurricane season. He knew that he would be busy all summer. Perhaps vainly, he wondered if the Federal money that the radio host was talking about might somehow come into play and help in his aspirational goals and career ambitions. Perhaps they might. If whackjob fringe-dweller Emerson thought money was being jettisoned out to help the "little guy," why couldn't that include Pete Demetri?

Looking up from the cab of the truck, he looked into the unnatural glow of the Red Roof Inn's neon sign and grabbed a paper bag that was stuffed into the console. Dinner for the night: a hoagie, a Boost! soda, and some abomination of a bakery dessert.

He would have hours to waste away watching the premium cable that the hotel boasted, fully abusing his air conditioning privileges in the room that Mr. Z was paying for, as they were officially on a job that called for such accommodations. Leaning forward to exit the vehicle, he shifted for a half a second and sat staring at the red lights. It was "unnatural," because it wasn't the crimson of a sunset or even of blood, it was artificial and teetering towards psychedelic, like the artistic gore in an Argento movie. A bad dream migraine of an effect only hinting at the true color of red.

In another lifetime, in a decade with less (or more) red tape and regulations, perhaps there would be three or four other trucks out here besides Pete, signaling a dozen other technicians and workers kicking back after a long day in the field. But between the union issues and other labor frustrations, tonight he was alone. Tomorrow, he would start the day venturing into the Pines, the natural world of this place holding its breath as it began its most tumultuous cycle of the seasons, equally on his own. Pete thought that the time out here wouldn't be a waste if he could learn something. Existing within this stasis of the eternal summer, of not having a solid career and not having much going on socially, his thoughts lingered vaguely on what he wanted out of it all. If he came away with some money and a story to tell, hell, that might just be enough.

TWO

When all was said and done, the line that Pete was responsible for would run about twenty-five miles from somewhere in the heart of the Pine Barrens inland towards the river, terminating in Burlington. Before all of the excitement swirling around current events, a completed line was run from Atlantic City towards this hub in the woods that now served as their starting point. If level heads had prevailed and temperaments remained professional, the same crews that had completed that first half of the track would have just kept rolling and likely could have finished this whole to-do without the threat of hurricane season messing things up and potentially causing delay after delay. Time would tell. Pete couldn't yet be bothered. He could go at his own pace, Mr. Z told him as much. They were both on the clock of a handful of state agencies, tossed around when looking for simple answers to questions like a neglected stepchild. Mr. Z genuinely laughed when Pete offered the comparison. It was the little things.

True to form, embracing the whole "take

your sweet ass time" approach, Pete's assignment today would be to head out in the work truck and take pictures of the mile markers for the sake of the project's ongoing spec detail and completion folio. There would only really need to be four or five pictures taken: the beginning, middle, and end, with alternate angles on the endcaps. But Mr. Z had given him enough film cartridges to make a damn flip-book if he had been so enthused. The bulky Polaroid camera was easy enough to operate and Pete thought about how often he had pined for just such a device as a kid. He had grown up another hour or so south and closer towards the river, towards the cities, rather than towards the coast and the more-picturesque locales. That didn't mean that the kid never had wanted to capture artsy glimpses of his youth.

In recent years, he might have gotten himself into a few bouts of trouble and petty criminality, but before that, living outside and rarely finding himself in his own bed at night meant that he was growing up properly, or at least that was what he told himself. No, you won't find many tourist brochures or travel agents singing the praises of places like Vineland, New Jersey or the mobile home community he grew up in, or the warehouse where he got his first summer job. But the night skies that he breathed in during those same seasons and the trails that he found himself lost in on the weekends, well, if they were half as pretty as he had remembered, Pete thought that he could make others, make outsiders, see the beauty in it that he had so sorely felt. That's why he always wanted a camera or something to document it all. Showing was a lot easier to do than trying to convey through words, especially when the medium was a dirty kid in overalls or flannel that never really properly fit his figure.

No, Pete never had a camera to call his own, but in high school and in the few openings for extracurriculars he had time for during vo-tech, he had taught himself to process and develop film. The stray teacher or instructor that assisted him was always encouraging and shared his appreciation for the medium. They said that Pete could take a mean picture, and they meant it. Not that he thought there would be many opportunities for landscapes or glamor shots today, but knowing what he did, contrasted to the automatic nature of the Polaroid camera that was shifting in the passenger seat next to him, he thought it would be a breeze. It was almost too-easy compared to those hours he had spent in a dark room, screwing up his eyes and almost chemically burning himself into a trip to the ER.

Of course, there were ulterior motives to Pete's enthusiasm for this otherwise-nothing portion of the assignment. Starting from the beginning of the proposed route, the utility work would be commencing less than an hour away from Stockton College, the same college where his high school sweetheart Maggie was currently in her second year. The chances of actually running into her hummed near a comfortable zero, but just being in the same vicinity as her had appealed to him. He could have, maybe should have, written or even called her and maybe try to arrange to have lunch or something. Go for a late morning walk between classes. But he didn't. Perhaps being in the same area code was the mental prodding enough for him to stop being a self-proclaimed coward and reach out again. She had asked him to before. Maybe another day, maybe another time when he didn't bear the grease marks of work on his hands and cheeks and when their ride to whatever destination they might have chosen wasn't the rattling, huffing beast he was currently driving.

Maggie had certainly been willing to hold on a little longer, but Pete felt something close to shame. She deserved more, or so he said, and thought that she could meet someone with the same career goals or academic ambitions that she held. They had both laughed at this conversation early one summer, a few years ago, until she realized that he was clumsily stumbling through an earnest thought. Maybe having consistently worked and having saved up some money now might bolster Pete's resolve to stop being a, in his words, whiny bitch, when it came to being honest with the young woman he claimed to love, but that was still a distant bridge to cross. He didn't risk crashing the truck by reaching for it, but he was reminded of the picture she had sent him that first summer she had gone away, still paperclipped inside the cover of the everywhere-notebook that currently sat on the floor of the passenger seat of the truck. The notebook had survived a handful of jobs, the end of his high school career, and multiple job training workshops in his path towards an apprenticeship. Maybe the same notebook would one day see him and Maggie together again. It was feasible, if he could only get out of his own way for once. Pete could never actually know this (unless he actually spoke to her), but she was always open to the call and always took her time looking through her mail, expecting something that never came.

The area before the long drive towards the college was quiet. There were a few gas stations and the roadhouse bar, with not much else in between. Not until you got closer to the shore, at least. Pete had a nearly photographic memory when it came to South Jersey and recalled the exact turnoff he needed to take to get to the mouth of the utility path that he and his crew would spend the next however many months (or years) working on. Even with all of the mental trepidation that went into resolving himself to drive to the town where his former paramour now lived, once he had gotten to the site of the original utility path, taken the pictures in the lonely, endless pines, and got back in his truck, he realized, stupidly, how quickly the whole endeavor came and went. Without anything to do in the area, he could now drive back along the route, almost along the way he came, except diverted further south to follow the trajectory of the utility path. Pete stared at the one side entrance of the college's campus as he sat at a stop sign. Maggie could be within a thousand feet of him at this very moment and she would never have known that he visited. He clicked on his blinker and pulled away from Stockton.

The towns that he passed through along the route were somehow even more desolate than the area surrounding Stockton College. One featured a gas station that looked decades-abandoned with a general store attachment that was equally neglected. Pete eyed his dashboard to stave off a growing fear of running out of fuel out here in the Pine Barrens and the sheepish call he would have to make to Mr. Z once he managed to track down a working phone. Fortunately, he had miles to go before that would become even an inkling of a concern.

Parking the truck, he uselessly gazed back the way he came, impossibly looking for the college town he had driven away from for about a half an hour. He knew it was a futile effort, but still tried to connect the physical trip he had made and the geography and math that he was relying on. The map and his work tools told him that he was in the right place, and he knew that he was, but he wondered how the hell he would have done this job even a hundred years ago. Hell, even a decade ago. For a moment his thoughts strayed away from the career ambitions he was currently aligned with and thought about the people on a different pay-grade that were making these calculations and using these maps, satellite images and coordinates and telling people like him, with a point and click, where to go dig, where to go chop down a tree, where to spend an afternoon in the sun. The money was good, but Pete thought that he would get stir crazy sitting in an office all day, doing just that. Maybe one day once his body began to give out. He coughed once and chided himself for allowing the opportunity for such a premonitory omen to afford itself. He chuckled and muttered a *fuck that* to himself.

Pete dug into his boots and pulled his socks up and over his work pants to account for the countless bloodsucking ticks that dwelled in the tall grass. He knew it was an outrageously goofy fashion, but decided not to hazard the diseases the deer ticks could carry. He was wearing long sleeves and a hat to avoid sunburn, the least he could do was basic protection for the stuff on the inside, too. He took one last look at the map before refolding it and sticking it in the front lapel of his overalls. Pete figured he must have been a sight, awkwardly stepping over the sandy hills and getting caught on the bushes as he blazed a trail armed with only his free hand and a Polaroid camera. After walking for about fifteen minutes, he thought that he might have made a mistake. He could no longer hear any sounds of traffic from the rural highway. After standing in place and looking around his perimeter for a few moments, he finally found salvation in the form of an orange flag about forty feet ahead.

Compared to the initial walk in, the rest of the trip was a breeze. He could see the cleared path diverging out from the flag in either direction and wondered how long it would have taken him to walk it on foot. It was not yet wide enough for the truck, and who knows how many muddy sinkholes lie in wait in either direction. Maybe after some more passes are done it could be traversable in a work vehicle. It would have to be, eventually. But that was months away at the earliest.

As he primed the camera and readied himself

to take the picture, Pete caught his breath and felt dizzy. A single bead of sweat rolled down his face from under his hat and he blinked. He was genuinely cold, momentarily chilled to his core, out here in eighty degree weather. Stumbling once before catching himself, he looked in either direction. The paths in either direction, east and west, suddenly felt a million miles long, the ocean on one end and a timeless void across the continent and off the surface of the earth, out into space, beyond. The vertigo of the moment gripped him and Pete felt that if he had fallen, he would somehow skew the axis of this path cut into the forest and throw the balance of the entire universe into disarray and disaster. Something broke the spell, like the sound of a bottle cap being snapped off a disturbed bottle of Coke, and Pete turned. A branch had broken behind him and although it was barely after midday, the dense throng at knee-level of the pygmy pines shrouded whatever woodland creature it was that was investigating Pete's trip as it made its escape. The animal bounded off into the woods and that gave him all the time he needed to refocus himself and actually breathe. He told himself that he needed to drink more water on these errands. The sugary shit was messing with him. He wondered if he was dehydrated.

He took a few more looks around and decided that he was no longer about to have some sort of anxious episode out here in the pines. Pete took the photograph of the trail marker without further issue and made his way back to his truck.

As he climbed into the cab and turned his keys, the voice of the professor came through the radio of the truck. Serendipitously, Pete would be heading in the direction of the station for his next and final stop. He glanced at the time and wondered if the show would still be broadcasting when he got to the area. He almost hoped that it wouldn't be and calculated how he could milk as much time as reasonably possible before his inevitable arrival. Allowing the truck to run a bit and cool him off, he ignored the open can of soda in the console and reached across to the bottle of water that had been rolling all over the floor during his day's drive. As he pulled it back, he picked up the familiar notebook that had been its dust-bound companion.

Pete drank almost half of the bottle in his initial swig and felt its relief, although he could taste the faint spell of plastic that lingered. He didn't know how old the bottle was, but was grateful for the water nonetheless. He recapped the bottle and dropped it onto the passenger seat. Still holding the notebook, he turned its cover flap over. There on the inside, of course, was the picture of Maggie. It was a Polaroid. He wondered for a moment how long it would take to fade. He had done the bare minimum in keeping it preserved, hadn't he?

21

THREE

Being able to dip between seldom-visited locations in the woods was a perk of the job. But to end today's run, Pete had to stop near the station where the utility trail terminated. Before he could escape without dealing with anybody, his worst nightmare came true. Standing in the parking lot of the radio station in the woods, he obtained the photographs he needed to take on this trip and was halfway back to his truck when he heard the sliding of a metal-framed door and the hurried, excited steps of a stranger. As if they were old friends, or as if the professor was the paparazzi, Joel Emerson almost tackled Pete as he came into proximity of the man and his work truck. Excusing himself, he remembered the normality of introductions and to, perhaps, explain why he was so excited to see him there in the parking lot.

"Exciting things, right?" the professor said.

"Uh," Pete nodded. "That's right, but I have to... throw some cold water on the excitement, Mr. Emerson-"

"Joel! Young Joel Emerson!" the old man laughed.

"Joel... you likely won't see any tangible changes

for... for a couple of years, at least."

"No, I understand that!" he waved a hand away. "But knowing that improvements and a boost to our broadcasting range are on the way, well, that's great news for our investors!"

As if on cue, a sheet of rusted siding fell from the exterior of the radio station, the wood underneath long-ago rotted away with water damage and wear.

"Er," Joel scratched his neck. "Potential investors, and all."

"Sure, Mister... sure, Joel," Pete corrected himself.

"Either way, thank you," the professor said, looking for something in his tweed jacket's pockets. "Here, take this, just in case you need to get in touch."

The professor handed Pete a business card. Pete had expected it to belong to the radio station, but it still detailed his contact information and office location at Stockton College.

"Don't mind all that business about the college, the mail and calls are still directed my way," he said with another somewhat obnoxious laugh.

Pete nodded and put the card inside his notebook's flap-folder pocket. It wasn't quite late enough for dusk yet, but the presence of a coming storm was looming, casting this portion of the pines in a dark gray overcast, a sick mimicry of an evening's dark. He never minded the rain, but found a renewed appreciation and fear for electrical storms due to his line of work. Though, with it being quitting time, the prospect of a gentle rain at night sounded appealing, if it would last. The professor seemed to detect his wandering gaze, beyond the confines of the parking lot and the radio station, and towards the clouds. The property seemed to sit at the bottom of a bowl, the gentle inversion of a hill dipped into the earth. Even the lowest of the pygmy pines were above eye-level down here.

"Pete, it was a pleasure to meet you. Feel free to stop by for lunch or something when you need the air condition. I've got nothing but time to talk and lounge in my office here, my working retirement."

"Thank you-" Pete began. He was again cut off.

"You feel that though, right?" the professor said, looking away from Pete and up towards the tree line.

"Feel…?"

And wouldn't you know it: he did feel it. Whatever *it* was. There was the omnipresent charge of static and ozone before a thunderstorm, but it felt peculiar out here. Heavier, but softer.

"Ah, it almost feels like Halloween if you ask me," the professor said. Pete had no idea what he could have possibly meant. "The walls are thinner, energies are running high. The world is tired, eh? Perhaps a bit ill."

Pete just blinked at the old man and almost expected him to go prone on the ground and listen to the blacktop, as if it were whispering to him. Fortunately, he seemed to snap out of it.

"Better let you get moving on!" he said. "Again, nice to meet you, Pete. Don't be a stranger and tune in if you're in the area! Well, I suppose you'll be just that for the foreseeable future."

Pete just smiled, briefly, and nodded before getting into his truck and heading back towards the hotel.

There were a few more vehicles in the hotel's parking lot than there were over the weekend. Pete hypothesized that they must be other types of traveling workers or people trying to escape their social obligations at home. He then presumed that those two groups could likely have pretty significant overlap but chose not to think too deeply on the subject. Entering the room directly from the lot, he was pleased to see the bed he left in disarray this morning neatly cleaned up and made. There was a large manilla folder on the breakfast table with a sticky note stuck to it. In chicken scratch, it informed Pete that his boss, Mr. Z, had sent it over around noon. Receiving work mail in this manner was nothing new to Pete and he secretly felt that it held an air of high-professionalism to it, tiptoeing towards mystery and intrigue. He wondered if the cleaning staff member that dropped it off ever guessed what it was that Pete did that was so important as to receive mail directly and in this way. The reality was that they didn't really care all that much, but it was fun to pretend.

In the room's closet, where visitors usually stored their valuables in the safe or hung up their expensive clothes on the rack to remain crisp, Pete stored his project's binder. It was a simple thing, but unruly and thick. He moved it to the table and spread out the recently received folder's contents, his own notebook, and the now-opened binder, to get a feel for all of the progress that he had silently already made. The red line of the proposed utility path shone through the paper map that was laminated and stuck to the interior of the binder. Its wobbly, bleeding ink-blot path was already forming a memorable shape in Pete's mind, an arcing slash that he would be able to, one day, recreate blindly if he had a marker and a blank piece of paper.

The brief interaction with Emerson made itself, somehow, the most prominent event of the day and partially blurred the hours that Pete had spent in the sun. Willing himself to see through the parking lot conversation and retrace his own steps out along the trail, he reviewed the scribble of notes he had kept, while looking at the laminated map. Taking a blue pen, he notched a few locations that had stuck out. The arc of the utility line ran mostly parallel to a creek through the forest. In some areas, the creek was only a couple yards away. At the greatest distance, it was about a half-mile away, but then wound back towards the route. It was unlikely that this was a coincidence. The powers that be must have had a reason, or previous experience with the land, that they followed this natural trajectory so closely. If there was an engineering purpose for it, Pete was still ignorant as to why. He mentally noted that it might be something to pick Mr. Z's brain about. Maybe in a few years time, the explanation would be obvious, with however many more hours of training and study he planned to have under his belt..

While he could not determine the mathematical reasoning behind the parallel path, he had seen, himself and in person, the existing structures and natural quirks that needed to be recorded for the sake of the project's integrity. In the areas that the creek ran closest to the proposed utility line, there were concrete spillways running along the trail, seeming to gently dam the creek, the smooth tiles sloping down towards the water. If it had ever flooded, the water that could hinder their construction would hopefully flow back down towards the waterway. While not yet an issue, Pete could imagine the logistical nightmare that would follow if storms capable of floodwater became a mainstay within the next few years. Nothing in their preparation had indicated that this was possible, but stranger things have happened. Most of these concerns would melt away (or rather, flow away) once the utility poles were firmly in place. Snow melts, ice, floods… all made irrelevant once their charge was complete and suspended high up, over the ground, inorganic forests of their own making. It was just getting there first that was the current obstacle.

With his pen, Pete traced where the longest lengths of spillways and existing concrete path girders had been noted. The only other landmarks that stuck out to him were two reservoirs positioned north and south of the trail, about a mile in either direction from a fire watch tower on a hill. He marked these, as well. This would be an exercise that he repeated at least three more times this month, in hopes of not missing a single inch of man-made, existing detritus in the field. He hoped that Mr. Z would appreciate this attention to detail. The air conditioning in the hotel room kicked on and Pete was blasted with that damp smell of false atmosphere. He reached for the remote and turned on the television. The weatherman said that the rain would persist through the night and Pete smiled before looking back to his work, the table an organized disaster. He hoped that anyone would appreciate his attention to detail.

FOUR

It occurred to Pete that he was getting… perhaps a "hybrid" education on his path to apprenticeship. Through both his own experiences, the stories that Mr. Z had alluded to, and tales that his father had told him growing up, he knew that a lot of the job was "hurry up and wait" and that his schedules were not exactly up to him to establish. There was plenty of red tape, of funding concerns, of last minute engineering decisions that were out of his hands and out of his employer's control. The know-how that went into being a lineman was just one component of the broader scope of a project. There were a million variables that went into getting the work ready for the actual installation of poles, and later, their electrical components. Pete reminded himself that they were not even at that stage (specifically, he was not yet a lineman). Nonetheless, knowing of all of this, Pete was not prepared for how mind-numbingly slow his early career as a utility scab could feel on the day-to-day.

He assumed that if he lived during normal, "boring" times, whatever firm he belonged to would likely have a series of ongoing projects and that he would not be expected to wait around all the time, for what felt like most of the week. But he was unfortunate enough to live during interesting times. There were no rosters of current projects, just the slim pickings that Mr. Z could elbow his guys into on per diem contracts (while collecting what he called his "finder's fee") and the backlog of civil engineering projects that the state and counties needed to be done with the Fed's insistence. This was all done as quietly as possible. The multi-thronged approach of union strikes had put up a stone wall between the government's demand and labor's supply. Pete was sympathetic, but he needed to eat. He needed to learn. In all that time spent waiting around for the next folder from Mr. Z's office, the ugly thought did creep into his mind: would his being a scab potentially hinder his professional prospects in the future? They'd understand, right?

After the second full-length inspection of the trail, and having not heard from the office for about a week, he decided that he would still walk the line when the weather was pleasant. Hell, he was being paid for it, why not get a little exercise, he reasoned. His diet was still just above literal garbage and dirt, so he might as well stretch his legs. Even considering the health benefits, he wondered if this practice did not harbor a silent, subtle detriment.

After a few hours in the sun and walking along the pines, Pete realized just how… stagnant certain portions of the pines could be. He could not place the exact word that he was looking for, but walking in the sandy dirt and seeing miles and miles of scraggy, sickly-looking pine trees, he thought that this might be similar to being "snow blind," although he knew that that was not at all what he was feeling.

If you were in stretches of fallen snow in direct sunlight, it was like being at the beach without sunglasses and staring up at the bright sky all day. The rays would reflect right into your face and scorch your eyes, slowly, and over time, until you were actually in pain and temporarily blind. No, he was not feeling any physical pain or discomfort from the repeated scenery, the washes of green and brown, but it was quietly taking a mental toll. He was reminded of his fascination with the idea of deja vu as a child and asking his mom, countless times, what her theories on the sensation was. She at some point, before regaining her patience with the boy, told him that it was what mothers experienced when their children asked the same question every day.

There were times when he thought he was at a certain portion of the pines only to find that he had miscalculated by miles at a time. He was generally good with directions and the feel for the geography of an area, so these errors sat very heavily with Pete. Determined to not allow this growing concern fester, he insisted on bringing a handheld radio with him on these trips to help break up the monotony. He reasoned that walking on the otherwise silent trail repeatedly allowed himself to get too in his own head. Though it was an unpleasant realization, he optimistically told himself that at least he discovered the susceptibility to this dizziness now and not when urgent, pressing work matters were on the line.

After another morning with no word from Mr. Z, Pete drove to the trailhead and began another walk, a bit earlier than he usually would. He was amazed to be able to see the morning dew in the pines. For just a moment, he had to do a double take when he thought he had seen frost in the woods, a layer gently coating ferns that had grown at the base of a healthier, "normal" looking pine tree. Rationalizing it as a trick of the early morning light, the sandy, glassy soil, and his give-or-take eyesight, the confusing image was dispelled. It was the middle of summer. There was not any frost to be found in this hemisphere, at least not at this altitude. Pete imagined himself suddenly breathing out a puff of visible, wintertime air and chuckled. He might be dressed for the much more mild weather, but he would experience no such break in the heat. He was not that fortunate.

He was proud of his hypothesis, nodding along to the rock station he had been listening to for the last forty minutes. There was no trace of that dizziness or deja vu he had felt so often on previous journeys. The music, an outside source of thought, was the only steadying hand he needed to traverse this path and not get lost in his own meditations. Of course, as if to punctuate how he saw himself and his own luck against the uncaring cosmos of reality, after about another twenty minutes or so, the telltale bloom of static began interfering with his radio. The station he had tuned to must have been from further up north, near the shore and city but of course not from those within his own proximity. New York, not Philadelphia. The ritzy beaches, not Down the Shore. No big deal.

Pete started fiddling with the tuner in hopes of finding another rock station that he could pick up out here in the middle of nowhere. There were a few hits, but they were golden oldies and he was not feeling particularly nostalgic this morning. He had finally found a station that was crystal clear and he scoffed, not believing that he had gone this long without encountering his wide-eyed friend from the parking lot ordeal.

Folks, it's young Joel Emerson on Your Local, the Eagle 1280 AM, ringing in the hour and wishing you a pleasant morning, and or a good night if you're anything like me in my prime and just finally hitting the hay as we speak, ha! What am I saying, THIS, this is my prime, baby! Now let me read you some of the niceties you all expect, with traffic and weather-

Pete had stopped on the trail and closed his eyes. Did he really want to listen to this deranged professor rattle on? If music had helped guide him along his way throughout the day, would the professor's show grant him the same luxury or exacerbate the issue? He gritted his teeth and rocked side to side for a moment before deciding that, even based on the non-committal encounter at the radio station, he did say he would check out the show for the professor's sake. How bad could it be? It would be fine. Fine, he turned the volume up and continued walking, the trail still not yet in direct sunlight, bathed in the cool gray-blue dawn, feigning twilight. The professor's voice continued.

Now, last week, we painted with an awfully broad brush, discussing Watchers and the world at large. A few of our particularly religious friends... listeners... had a few words to share with us afterwards. We love the feedback, both supportive and... and... well, let's just say excitable. We're reeling it back a bit this week, not so much for a global perspective, but for watchers, guardians really, of a certain geographic region. Whether it be woods, or mountains, or villages, we're looking into and talking about region-specific creatures and otherworldly entities whose interests may be beyond our purview. Coming up on the next hour, I have a dear friend of mine, a kind of jack of all trades, but journalist by profession, who spent some time out in West Virginia a few years ago and has quite a story to share, one pertaining to one of these… these, well, these monsters.

Think about it while I get the coffee on. Have you ever felt the presence of something out there in the woods with you at night? Have you ever seen something that you just simply cannot explain, an intelligence that is beyond human or animal, and one that you cannot describe?

Pete found the way that the professor meandered around getting to the point a tad irritating, but realized that might have been on purpose, what with it being a radio talk show. He had not felt the urge to immediately turn to a different station, so it could not be all that bad. If nothing else, the show did get him thinking a bit outside of the box. He had been so focused on getting situated with training and his job recently, there had not been much time or thought dedicated to the subtle, constant magic of existence that surrounded him. Hell, hadn't he mused on the beauty of South Jersey suburbia while reminiscing on the photography projects of his youth? Just because he was a bit older now did not mean that his eye or capability for that appreciation went away.   Perhaps it was just a bit more subdued now, put aside when other parts of him were forced to function, when the dull reality of survival was the environment in which he was forced to operate.

He had hit the quarter marker and turned back around to return to his truck, as there was not anything more for him to do on foot. This was still a part of his extracurricular time on the trail, so to speak. The sun had since risen and any hints of that imagined frost were now long gone, but the early morning light did paint the landscape in a fresh palette that Pete had not yet noticed or appreciated. Amidst the sandy browns and faded greens, he detected the faintest brushings of blue in the pines. Taking a deep breath, he paused and shuddered for a moment, feeling uncharacteristically cold for a fleeting moment. There, again, he imagined being able to see his breath and blinked to snap out of it.

Pete almost choked before stifling a surprised laugh. As his eyes focused, he saw not twenty feet away from him a thin, frail deer, out there alone. He had seen the creature head on, so the odd shape of the animal was foreign to him at first, an alien with bulbous eyes standing on two thin legs. But when its ears perked up and he noticed the disinterested chew of its mouth, his panic fled and he stood there, staring at the docile thing. Eventually, it turned to move and took one last look at the intruding human before disappearing into the brush. Pete blinked again before resuming his walk back on the trail. The creature's fur seemed to have been coated in glittering specks of that fabled, frosted morning dew and caught in the light before the animal had made its departure.

FIVE

After the fourth day of radio silence, Pete assumed that this time spent playing on house money was coming to an end. Either Mr. Z would call it, or the project itself would be put on hold, the powers that be finally deciding to stop skirting around the labor strike and let the work completely and wholly pause until a greater resolution was struck. Late last year, before the cold season, something similar had happened. It was one of the first gigs that Pete had spent time under at Mr. Z's direction.

The boss had said that no news was always good news, but in these interesting times it mostly seemed that the opposite was true. You'd be in near-constant contact with a field office when times were good and the work was consistent. But then their correspondence would drop off. No more daily phone calls. No more letters. No more package drops. Like some jilted lover, you'd slowly lose contact with the people holding your paycheck until finally they disappeared. The landline to their HQ would no longer connect and if you were lucky enough to live in the same zip code, a visit to the address revealed a dead-bolted door and unpaid bills piling up at an unkempt doorstep. In fairer times, there was legal recourse to pursue. There was no such luxury when you were a scab.

Deciding that he was going to make the most out of presumably dwindling time, Pete set out for one more paid morning hike. Instead of embarking redundantly from the threshold he was now so familiar with, he took the truck and parked near the midpoint of the path, that much closer to the radio station in the woods and the ever-smiling professor behind the desk. He did not intend to see the man or actually step foot on the property itself, but if he was justifying these walks as "checking on" the conditions of the utility route, he might as well do it justice and see if anything had changed since the last review.

The humidity was palpable. It was not nearly as sunny and cheerful as it had been earlier in the week and the sky held the constant threat of a looming thunderstorm. Pete did not think he would have much luck with the rock station on his radio this far out to begin with, but even the clearer signal of the professor's station was tainted with bitter chirps and bites of static every couple of seconds, hinting at the electrical storm that could begin any second, always hanging over the day, silent until it was not. The signal did seem to be getting more stable as he inched closer to the station, but Pete could not help but wonder why the hell he was out here in the first place. If his intuition was right, and all professional and observational metrics indicated that they were, he might be out of a job by this time tomorrow. Why wasn't he going back to Mr. Z's shop? Or scoping out a job board somewhere in the area? Perhaps there was some truth in the professor's words about these woods, that they felt *different* and at this time, different felt comforting. Not reliable, but at least it was there.

Pete was caught up thinking through those lofty thoughts that had been shared in the parking lot. The air had felt heavy, as if the woods were about to speak. On the surface, that doesn't sound particularly pleasant or reassuring. It inched towards being creepy. That did not really line up with the current feelings of contentment. He should be thinking about tomorrow, worried about the immediate future, but he was just fine out here on the sandy trail. He allowed himself to avoid confrontation with these thoughts and instead let them drift and smother his surroundings and listened to the people speaking through the radio, just a few miles away. They were apparently students from Stockton College, presumably belonging to a previous class of the professor's.

-and it's all there in the book. I've put in three requests for the library to carry it, and they've finally approved it the last time. Even the most line-in-the-sand skeptic would have to agree it's a little weird and get the chills over the fact that the creature was some sort of bad omen for Point Pleasant, a girl's voice said.

Yeah, it was very entertaining. But the author seemed to think pretty dang highly of himself, right? That he was some sort of linchpin in all of this, tracking clues and flirting with every quiet, pretty lady from Ohio to Maine, a boy questioned.

That's just it, though. He doesn't think he was a catalyst to it. He knows he's just some guy. What he's trying to say, what I think he's been trying to get across is that, is that... that those greater patterns in the world are discernible, they are out there to be found by any Joe Schmo. Just because you're witness to something incredible doesn't mean that you were the intended audience. It doesn't mean it was necessarily meant to be viewed, at all. Maybe.

Well, that's a definitive answer, Linnie, the boy replied, and both speakers laughed.

Hey, I never claimed to be an expert. This is just what we like and read about, you know?

Of course, of course. So, that creature out in Ohio,

sorry. Out in West Virginia. If we were to put it on the weird creature's family tree. Let's say the spectrum is... Bigfoot on the far, far left and aliens are on the far right. Where does this creature sit?

That's a good question... for our listeners, let's give some more detail to this scale. As a familiar centerpoint, let's say our Jersey Devil would be somewhere in the middle then.

You think the Jersey Devil is between Bigfoot and aliens from outer space, Linnie?

Why wouldn't she be? In my personal opinion, and I could be wrong, people see the Bigfoot as a docile, lower-thought-process creature. A giant ape, silent protector of the forests. Aliens are sophisticated, potentially harmful, but highly intelligent and use technology. Those are the two ends of our scale. And who knows, perhaps I'm wrong and it's more of a circle than a line, but that's not the point of this conversation. I would still say the Jersey Devil is somewhere in between. A wild, uncivilized animal with claws and wings, sure. But with her birth being one of potentially demonic and sacrilegious origins, well, she's not just a skunk ape in the woods. There's an intelligence there, one that, if she exists, we probably can not possibly understand. Unless we spoke to it. And even then...

The professor then broke in: *I do not think we could entice the youngest Leeds child into our studio, unfortunately,* and soft laughter again emitted from the radio.

About once a minute, sharp static would cut the feed entirely and there would be silence for a few seconds after, the unknowing and unaffected broadcast continuing without acknowledging the interference. It was interference from outside the station. Although Pete was not convinced that the studio or the professor were really on top of their game (or ready for national syndication..) he assumed that they were keen enough to detect anything like that coming from their side of things. It was the coming electrical storms screwing with lesser pieces of equipment, like the handheld radio that accompanied him on these morning walks. Maybe it was a subtle signal from beyond to get a move on.

As he retraced the familiar steps, he thought about the creatures that the program hosts had been discussing. They were still pulling at the same thread, but the repeated disruptions had begun to irritate Pete and he lowered the volume on the radio until it was now almost inaudible. Everyone around here knew the story of the Jersey Devil, but any individual would have their own ideas about the other things that also went bump in the night. He was thinking about what those monsters thought of one another, if they, well, existed at all and if they had any notion of the others existing to begin with. What did they think of people? What about animals? Did they differentiate between humans, animals, and other weird in-betweens such as themselves? He was really caught up on something one of the hosts had said: (*maybe the tree of the unknown) is more of a circle than a line.* It was a compelling thought, though he did believe it to be a tad silly, picturing a Bigfoot-like creature communicating to a stereotypical little gray alien and giving it directions, after fixing a broken taillight on its flying saucer. He headed back to the hotel.

For once, there were communications waiting for him. Pete unwrapped the familiar folders and laid out everything that was sent his way, ignoring most of it to get to the brief, handwritten note on yellow paper that Mr. Z had always given him the rundown on. He was told that this would be his last night in the motel unless he really wished to stay on his own accord (and dollar) and that the project had almost been put on an indefinite hold. The fact that Pete had been "on the job" this entire time had kept it going. He couldn't help but smirk to himself. His little paid vacation had functioned as a professional gambit. Only he and Mr. Z knew that he was effectively doing nothing for the last week or two, but that was enough to convince whatever municipal clerk to shrug and say, "carry on, then," when he tried to call the shop and tell them to cease further work. Pete had his own eagerness to begin inching into the next steps of the project, but could appreciate his boss' objective outlook: who gives a fuck about progress, we're still getting paid during an industry-wide drought. He'd take the small victory when nothing much else was going on. There was just a slight change in plans as they pertained to his lodgings.

With the strikes still going on, public and state properties were considered closed, though Pete always asked himself how does one close a forest? With that being the case, there were not any paying visitors camping on the grounds or utilizing the rudimentary cabins in Wharton State Forest, where most of the western portion of the utility route would run through. In the package there were two rusty keys on a chain and a folded paper map showing Pete where his new, temporary digs would be. He would be staying in one of those shitshacks this summer, for however long the "secret" project continued to operate under the nose of the unions and inundated government agencies. The local municipalities wanted, no, needed this work done, eventually, and they were helping creep the ball towards the goal line until the powers that be got their acts together and then everyone could celebrate a job well done. Public service and public good, for the people. Or something.

The air conditioning in the motel room kicked on and he got a whiff of the damp but not entirely unpleasant cool air and took one last look around the room. He swept his few belongings into his own canvas bag and turned off the lights that he had left on since earlier this morning. The swift movement halted when he stopped, put his stuff on the end of the bed, and took a second to sit down and turn on the TV. He wanted to see what the weather was going to be like. As mildly exciting the prospect of checking out a cabin was, his enthusiasm was dampened a bit, no pun intended. For the next week, the southern half of the state would be experiencing rain and the storms that Pete's radio had forecasted this morning on the trail. There was a tropical storm brewing down the coast, as well. It may very well develop into the first hurricane of the season.

Well, he thought to himself. At least I'll still have a roof over my head. That counted for something.

SIX

The campgrounds at Wharton had seen better days, though Pete was not entirely sure if they were ever the image of tidiness, let alone luxury.

It was already later in the day when he arrived. With dusk falling, he killed the truck's light as soon as he was comfortably within the confines of the semicircle of sandy soil that acted as the small roadway into the community of shelters. There were at least six that he could see in the failing light. Off this access road, the dirt trail went back and then arced all the way back to the pavement. From there, you could see both access points, no more than four hundred feet from one another. But the semicircle went deep and was arranged as if it were a residential street, each cabin posted with its own mailbox. They weren't set up to receive regular mail, but people were so used to the niceties of home, Pete figured that if people were looking for a cabin in lieu of roughing it in the woods, they'd appreciate a familiar facade wherever they were staying.

In better times, a cheerful park ranger might visit every morning and leave pamphlets for the visitors. Maps to the closest fishing pond, anything detailing events happening in the area... that sort of thing. But so far, Pete only saw the early stages of disrepair. The cabins must have seen use within the last two years or so, but the first one he approached was already busted off its post and its metal carrier box was punctured in the center, as if something had stepped on it, with purpose. The keys that Mr. Z had left him might have had a number etched on them, but he couldn't discern any to save his life. He considered returning to the truck and using a light to further investigate, but he was already walking towards the second cabin before he could talk any sense into himself. Pete did not want to hazard any unnecessary light out here, as it was.

With the first two cabins not reacting to the key at all, he was at least temporarily motivated when the third lock accepted the keys, but then did not turn. A slight drizzle had started falling on him in the dark. The canopy of the taller trees had kept him dry thus far, but the small, scraggy pines that dotted the trail teased him in the diminished light, each one looking like a childhood goblin reaching out for his legs. It was too easy to spook yourself out there in the pines, especially without a light, and Pete was slowly losing any protective wit against this fear as he stepped off the small porch and began walking towards cabin number four. This one had brush from the taller trees on top, as if it had naturally begun to cover itself in treefall to blend in with the environment, albeit poorly. He thought to himself how stupid this was, leaving a light behind. But he was already past the apex of the semicircle. No matter how creepy or dark it got, he was at least now approaching the road again, and the safety of the truck.

As a matter of minor divine providence, it turns out that the keys belonged to cabin number four. It ended up being foolish to expect any correspondence from Mr. Z's office to be awaiting him. In hindsight, the post hole digger leaning on one of the pillars of the front porch should have been a dead giveaway. As Pete stepped through the screen door of the cabin, he inhaled months of cobwebs and sputtered in the dark, reaching out and lashing at the unseen net trapping him. He reached for a lightswitch and found himself patting the wooden wall. Oh, duh. He saw a small imitation kerosene lamp on the table and flipped it on. It was battery operated and only made it look old-timey. Pete was more impressed that in the whole state of things, this stupid battery-operated flashlight still held power, but he didn't further test his luck and jinx it by thanking it aloud.

The cabin itself was comfortable. Like the previous base of operations in the motel it too held a damp smell, but it was not quite the same. It was much closer to the outdoors and lord knows if the unstable structure had any leaks in its roof, or problem with groundwater, or if the half-sized refrigerator leaked, the whole nine yards. As soon as you entered, on the left sat a cot in the corner with a thin green, fleece blanket and paper-like pillowcase on a flat cushion. Pete slightly grimaced at this, not knowing how long it sat in this state and what kind of unknown visitors could have touched it. A slight rumbling of the thunder outside told him to deal with it and he devoted no further thought to the matter.

There was a small kitchenette area with a sink next to the fridge. There was a ceiling fan with a pull string switch and exposed lightbulb in the center of the ceiling. Through a dirty rear window, he could see the outhouse in the knee-high weeds out back. How quaint. He placed the folder with the auxiliary key and documents on the table and decided to roll the truck around before it got darker and even later.

He kept the lights low, idly at the parking level. Retracing the path he had just taken on foot in the safety of the cab was a breeze and Pete appreciated the familiarity that was growing with his new accommodations. Come daylight, he'd enjoy taking another morning walk in this small stretch of paradise, that was what he told himself. Parking the truck outside of cabin number four, he looked around and confirmed that he was pretty damn isolated. There may have been some Pine Barrens natives out there, miles away, but the closest known neighbors were about five miles away on the main road, and far enough away from this access road.

There was a serenity in the isolation, one that he found comforting. The spell was broken when an inhuman screech sounded from somewhere deep in the woods, from behind the cabin and the semicircle of other shelters. He froze, scanning the waist-high scrub pines for a discernible, watching, breathing figure. Pete couldn't tell how long he stood there, half out of the truck and staring into the gray-blue evening, half ready to abandon his post and drive home. When he could finally move again, he hefted a crowbar from the backseat of the truck. It would act as his security blanket for the night. When he finally slammed the door of the truck closed, the creeping discomfort melted away. A few small birds fluttered skyward from nearby. Assuming that they, too, were shocked into silence from whatever it was that made the noise, Pete was reassured if the sound of him and a door could wake them back up into reality.

"Probably a fox in heat... or a rabbit getting got," he muttered and turned towards his cabin.

Clumsily, Pete took the post hole digger from the porch and carried both it and the crowbar inside. The sun had now firmly set and he realized how important the lantern would be in case he needed to do anything outside for however long he remained in these lodgings. Though he was trying to lay low enough to not allow the truck's headlights to blow up his presence, he thanked no one in particular that silence wasn't as critical of an attribute to maintain out here in his covert operation. He sounded like a roadie barging through the one room building with the tools in stow.

Allowing himself a moment to catch his breath, Pete reassessed the cabin. The lantern glowed from the round table. The fridge hummed to itself. Realizing that he had additional access to electricity, he switched off the lantern and pulled at the drawstring he saw hanging from the ceiling. A wobbling ceiling fan began tilting as an unshaded bulb flared to life. Pete could see the dust and dirt falling on the room and his scant belongings, but like the matters concerning his bed, he tried to ignore it. It was something. It was some white noise that would hopefully make sleeping out here not seem nearly as vulnerable. That was something that he had always balanced. How much isolation was a relief and how much did it invite danger? Whatever the case was out here in the Pine Barrens, he had hoped that he could simply sleep through it either way.

The door was locked. All the work stuff was quarantined on or around the single table and the ceiling fan buzzed in tandem with the refrigerator. Pete took off his boots near the door and drew the canvas blinds on the four windows of the cabin. He had decided to protect this budding sense of comfort and avoid any distractions spurred on by horror movies he had grown up watching. It was hard enough to get the sound of that screech from before out of his mind. Realizing he had no television to fall asleep to, he felt a punch of anxiety in his gut only for it to void a moment later when he saw a bright red radio sitting on top of the fridge. Even if the thing didn't work, he still had the one he carried with him every day at work. He had his happy little tools to distract himself with.

Cursing, he realized had to use the facilities and wash up before he could hope to sleep. He undid the routine he had just completed and took a deep breath before unlocking the door. Of course there wasn't any monster waiting for him on the porch. Of course there was nothing waiting for him as he stepped off the wooden step and retrieved his personal radio from the truck. He had almost given himself a heart attack at the sound of the wood straining and releasing under his foot, but he laughed as he placed the device on the table and turned to go visit the outhouse for the first time. He had wished he could have done so during the daylight, but nature called and he did not quite feel like breaking in his new accommodations by pissing off the front porch. Pete was comfortable there, but not quite that comfortable. It would have been different if he was camping, but this was a home of sorts. He even had a mailbox, for Christ's sake.

The outhouse, of course, smelled horrendous. It might have been a small blessing that he couldn't see what kind of monstrosity and abandonment of decency sat within the booth. But once again, nothing grabbed him from the dark, nothing spoke to him in the stall, and he had exited almost as quickly as he had entered, feeling relieved. As he shut the door to the outhouse, he heard that familiar wooden creak that signaled someone stepping off of the front porch of the cabin. Whatever had caused the noise was separated only by the cabin itself, the dark, and the ten or so feet of space that it would take Pete to round the corner.

No footsteps followed. No animal or man's breath could be heard near the truck. Pete just stood outside the outhouse and waited. Stupidly, he had neither of the tools he had brought inside the cabin. It was just him and the battery operated lantern, which he now felt betrayed him out here in the dark. He clicked it off and continued to wait. It was summertime in the Pine Barrens and Peter Demetri felt like he was freezing. In the dark, he thought that he could see his breath and in bewilderment almost turned the light back on to confirm this insane hypothesis. The only reason he chose not to was because he recalled why it was he was straining his hearing and listening to the dark, standing alone in the woods. He was listening to ascertain whether or not he was in present danger.

He had two options. He could stand there and wait until whatever it was crept back into the shadows and then into his proximity and did whatever it was that it was planning to do, or he could rush towards the house and hopefully past this intruder, and into the safety of the lit cabin. Four walls. He could at least shut himself in and reassess what to do. The latter was the objectively better option, but the primal fear that he felt had bolted him in place and chilled him to his core. It was then that the shrieking made its second appearance of the night, this time much closer to Pete, maybe a hundred yards away in the dark, and high up, just beyond the outhouse. He ran.

There was nothing waiting for him on the porch. He didn't see anything near his truck as he sprinted into the cabin and slammed the door shut, the screen rattling in its frame as he swung it open and it fell closed behind him and the heavy door he was now locking.

When the adrenaline finally tapered off and Pete again felt the humidity of the natural world, he calmed his breathing and tried to laugh the whole deal off, forcing a series of unnatural chuckles. He hadn't removed his boots this time, not yet, but was trying to again wind down as he had done before. He left the ceiling fan on, but gently unscrewed the lightbulb so he could hopefully rest easier in the dark. The bulb was not yet too hot to the touch. Now that the moment had passed, he realized how tired he was and was genuinely finding himself amused.

He clutched his personal radio like a teddy bear and turned it on. Pete would have accepted anything to fill the natural silence (sans electrical humming from the nearby appliances) but was, of course, greeted by the voice of the professor, locked in for a nighttime block.

Gooooood evening, South Jersey! You're listening Your Local, the Eagle 1280 AM–

Pete had actually laughed at this, continuing his slightly maniacal streak. Now his boots were finally off and he laid down on the sagging cot, its rusted springs creaking with every shift. He turned down the volume of the radio, but did feel appreciation for the familiar voice. The ceiling fan had helped cut down on the smothering heat of the pines and humidity of the nearby swamps and storms. The gentle rain picked up in the night and Pete heard the precipitation that broke through the canopy falling on the cabin. Sleep did finally come, eventually. He had placed the radio on the floor near where his head lay on the cot. The cabin did have its charm. Combined with the rain, the soothing songs and voices he heard on the radio, and the constant hum of the ceiling fan, Pete found rest. The last thing he saw before he drifted off was the distant shape of the outhouse, visible through the nightfall and the dirty window in the rear of the cabin.

SEVEN

With the dawn of a new day and hours between the excitement of last night and himself, Pete awoke and settled back into the relative boredom of the job. Rereading the materials that Mr. Z had left him and looking outside, he noticed the dozen post markers on the side of the cabin, stacked and covered in a tarp like unnaturally smoothed logs prepared for firewood. Sometime this week, he would meet up with Mr. Z or other nameless coworkers and get a hold of a wheelbarrow and even more of these post markers, but this would be a good start. It had been almost chilly outside when he had started, but after moving the markers from the side of the cabin and into the bed of his work truck, Pete was sweating as the sun had finally fully risen.

The entire southern half of the state was going to be damp, but Pete wanted to at least get this load of post markers out as a sign of the project's slow, incremental progress. He secured a strap to the previously loose pile of logs when voices made him pause. He turned, straining his hearing, his gaze following the arc of the dirt road that made up his current neighborhood. Through the haze and thin expanse of forest of the semicircle, he saw another truck park outside of cabin number two. They weren't a construction crew, that was made obvious by the bright orange hunting gear that gave their business away. There were two men. It looked like they both wore camouflage, with one wearing a bright orange hat and the other wearing the neon vest over his clothes. Pete looked out to the larger road, already set to leave for the day, but decided to go make his presence known. He reasoned it might help both parties out to know they had neighbors. Last thing he needed was one of them getting drunk and shooting him next time he needed to use the outhouse…

"Morning, guys," Pete started, approaching the men who were unloading things out of their truck.
One flinched and looked around, the other almost dropped a large cooler that was being dug out of the open tailgate.
"Jeez, mister," the one who flinched laughed, now seeing Pete. "Scared the shit out of me."
"Erik," the one struggling with the cooler gasped. "Erik, the cooler-"
Erik flinched again and turned to help his companion. Pete saw the lid pop momentarily and that the two avoided losing however many precious beers to the mishap. Calamity averted, they were all

in better spirits.

Pete had described his last month of work to the two, Erik and Carl. They were hunters who also had some contacts on the inside of the currently striking public workers and decided to take advantage of the unsupervised amenities. Pete really didn't care one way or another, but his wandering mind allowed him to put his foot in his mouth for him.

"You know, I've seen a bunch of 'no hunting' stickers up, all around here," he said, waving his arm towards the woods. Erik grimaced and looked at his feet, taking his hat off and dusting it once.
"Well," Erik said. "We'll just fish then, won't we, Carl?"
Carl nodded, the niceties draining away. Now having a few moments to rest, he hefted the cooler once more and moved it towards the open door of the cabin.
"I didn't mean anything by it, guys," Pete said, simply. "Just that the sheriff probably won't give a shit about people being in the state grounds when they're closed… but they'll probably start snooping if they hear live rounds."
"No, no," Erik nodded. "You're right, kid. It's good to keep us honest."

With peace reestablished, Pete gave a slight wave and turned back to his cabin to head out for the day.

About halfway back up the road, he heard another trunk get dropped out of Erik and Carl's truck, a heavy metallic sound muffled by the sandy soil of the Pine Barrens.

No matter where Pete was starting his day from, he found himself getting further used to all of these tracks in the Pines. The radio station and most main roads towards the utilities route were now firmly taking place as landmarks in his mental command of the geography. His thoughts were drifting towards the cabins, his new neighbors, and what would happen if anyone showed up and tried to give any of them grief. They all had their own reasons to be there, but he wasn't quite sure how much permission they actually had to be there in the eyes of the law. Would Mr. Z bail him out? He shook his head and didn't really like the options. While the cabin was a fun little excursion, filled with adventure and just a dash of anxiety, the appeal of the motel accommodations kept resurfacing. Maybe it would be worthwhile to bite the bullet, take a hit from his salary, and just pay for his own lodging. There was no way it was feasible to commute over an hour towards his current apartment in Central Jersey every day for this job, no matter what it meant to his career route. He would dwell on it and think of something, if he wasn't prematurely booted from the campsite before a decision could be made.

It wasn't really the strangers showing up that made a mental cloud of the day. He actually thought they seemed like friendly people. Just now being back in the land of the living, Pete felt off. Maybe he was still tired from all of the adrenaline that he was subjected to last night. He never really determined what those shrieks in the canopy of the woods could have been. He had offered rationalities to himself, but he was a pisspoor outdoorsman and an even worse comforting voice of reason. Pete didn't want to admit it, but there was one hypothesis he had for his unpleasant mood.

The work itself was simple and he was done by noon, due to his limited supplies. He had parked and lugged out a handful of the post markers each trip. Even with the rainfall, the holes he had previously inspected were all still intact and accepted their marker. He tapped them into the ground a few times with the spade he carried and moved to the next one. Once again, as he returned to the truck, he was sweating, but not particularly tired. He sat in the cab of the truck and allowed himself to get cooled off. Without ceremony, he read through the notes regarding this phase of the project for the hundredth time and then flipped towards the front pouch of the notebook and looked at the picture of Maggie.

Looking in the rearview mirror, he wiped

away the sweat with his forearm and fixed his hat hair. It was pretty awkward, but he reached down for the Poloroid and then hefted it up against the steering wheel, stretching out his hands as far as he could. He decided to snap a picture of himself making a silly face and would mail it to her like a postcard. Maybe he would write on some of the abandoned literature he had found regarding the cabin. Write a letter or something describing the spooky encounters on the first night and his new neighbors. Maybe if he did get arrested at some point, it would help for a loved one to know exactly where he was. It was a silly line of thought that amused him.

So that's what he did. On the way back towards the cabin, he grabbed an envelope and a handful of stamps from the post office he had seen on the thoroughfare. The place must have been about twenty feet across in every direction and barely had any running electricity. He thought that the place might have actually been shuttered when he pulled in and saw its condition close up. He only followed through when he saw an ancient man open the front door and shuffle away down the road lacking any sidewalk.

Pete could not help but think about the few friends he still thought about from high school and the even fewer ones he grew up with. What were they up to? Most of them were probably still in Jersey, as well. There were at least one or two that were absolutely down the shore with family, or making use of a particularly affluent neighbor that owned property down there this time of year. He wasn't jealous at the prospect of the vacation plans, but at the idea of having some company. As he pulled back into the sandy, secret neighborhood in the woods, saw that his new friends had gone off on their own adventures, and now sat outside the cabin meant for one, Pete realized that that was a huge reason for his growing discomfort and the blooming anxiety that crept towards his throat at every hour of the day. He was feeling incredibly lonely.

EIGHT

As a kid, sunny days were every part as enjoyable as the stereotype let on. Being outside and on his own so much, Pete appreciated the mild weather. Later on, towards the end of high school and the culmination of his being constantly surrounded by others, he cultivated an appreciation for the inclement and the isolation that it spurred, as well. Of course, this had begun to wane as his daily professional endeavors had begun to rely on a cooperative climate. It was an ebb and flow between portions of his life, professional and personal. What made him comfortable versus what secured his financial well-being. While it should have resulted in a well-rounded individual, the reality of the matter seemed to have done the opposite. All of this had culminated in an individual leaving young adulthood who was never quite comfortable in any given temperature or surrounding. It was not so much as arrested development as it was being a stranger in a land that was supposed to be familiar.

Watching as day turned to early evening,

Pete had somehow abated the relentless clouds of mosquitoes that seemed to smother the state this time of year. It might have been the citronella candle he had burning on the small table next to him on the porch, or maybe his general air of "please leave me alone" was enough. Though he didn't think the vile creatures were that emotionally intelligent and he smirked to himself thinking about it.

After preparing a simple meal from the fridge in the kitchenette area and returning to his place on the porch, he wondered what the hunters were going to do for their evening meal and was already getting envious at the imagined scents that their campfire and presumed grilling would elicit. Even though he just ate, Pete's stomach growled in jealousy. Hell, if they did end up doing some rudimentary barbecuing, maybe he would shed some of his shell and go and say hey (and potentially join them in whatever they were cooking over an open flame). He was physically dry, but the isolation and constant dreariness (not to mention the unyielding humidity throughout all hours of the day, now stagnant) gave him the chills. Everything felt like an unpleasant gray and blue and, now that the sun had set, black. Without a TV out here, he longed for the primitive allure of an open fire. He had exhausted his enjoyment of listening to the radio for the day. Pete leaned forward and looked around the front lot of the cabin. There wasn't really anywhere convenient to make a fire of his own. Maybe he would clean some space tomorrow when he could see.

Movement had caught his eye, but it was not anything alarming or existentially concerning. Not like hearing that screeching the other night. Out on the path that constituted the road through the "neighborhood" of cabins, Pete watched a small caravan of forest wildlife coming from the forest and going out towards the roads meant for humans. It very well could have been composed entirely of rabbits, but Pete swore he saw a few similarly sized and shaped (but different) animals, like squirrels and chipmunks in the mix. Did they usually interact, let alone get along with one another like that? Feeling like a Disney princess, Pete wished he had his camera that was currently sitting on the floor of his work truck on hand to capture the moment, not considering how critically dark and impossible it would be to capture the shot properly.

The procession only lasted for a few minutes and the smile stayed for a little while longer on Pete's mouth. His expression faded and fell into a curious, neutral stare when his thoughts lingered towards the nature of the odd scene. Animals don't just befriend one another like people would. Why were they uncharacteristically cooperating and moving in tandem? Were they… fleeing from something?

Pete started when the sound of a large branch breaking snapped him to attention, but he caught his breath when he realized it was the sound of his neighbors across the way finally arriving home after their day of activities in the woods. His concerns regarding the forest life were momentarily calmed when he realized that perhaps the rabbits were just running away from the metaphorical Lenny and George, loudly and belligerently stomping through their home. It was only his mind playing tricks, but Pete thought he could smell the booze on them from here. He clicked his tongue and smirked, slowly shaking his head. He might try to be a little social tonight, but was already planning his escape route in the likely chance that they were obnoxious drunks. Their self-produced fanfare that heralded their arrival told Pete that it was likely that they were.

He gave them some time to settle in, and to give himself the chance to see if they were going to even be acting agreeable to an outsider tonight. For all he knew, they would retire to their cabin, kill their kerosene lamps and flashlights and call it a night. That did not appear to be the case as Pete watched a campfire begin to breathe life, first as an ember in the blue dark, then as a miniature bonfire. Apparently, their cabin's property was much more agreeable than his. If only there was some concierge to field such complaints. No such relief for people living laying low. Taking a deep breath, Pete stood and began walking towards the fire across the way.

They noticed him before he could say anything. It was like they were longtime friends and they shouted and hooted when he became visible in the dark. The hunters ushered him in, offering a seat on the only-slightly damp log opposite themselves around the fire. Their obnoxiousness was as comforting as the fire on this night, so closely removed from those oddly penetrating feelings of loneliness Pete was musing on only an hour before. Perhaps these feelings were lifted because another component of his earlier speculation was correct: they were grilling all sorts of wonderful, terrible foods on the open flame. The hunks of meat they pulled from a previously unseen cooler (not to be confused with the beer cooler) were reminiscent of childhood family affairs in backyards of people Pete did not know the name of. They were birthday parties and Fourth of Julys and simpler times dashed with the rambunctious laughter of perfect strangers that felt like friends and he was nodding along and he was tired and he was content.

The hunters gave Pete the usual stories and

spiels they offered any newcomer or stranger in their travels. These minor rituals generally tended to be at smoke-laden old man bars around the gut of the state or at the odd fishing competition they'd splurge a bit for down the shore. There were all of the usual suspects: ladies they knew back in the day, bucks with antlers that could gore a tractor's tire, that time that Erik pulled a shark onto the deck of a pontoon they rented for a day of catfish fishing in the bay. Pete was once again reminded of those anonymous neighbors and relatives from his childhood and their equally unbelievable but enjoyable stories.

After an hour or so of uninterrupted exaggerations, Pete let some of the more grandiose stories land without argument, but could not shake a few details about the men's hunting stories and the whole situation at hand. The time of year, their business out here in the pines…

"Say, guys," Pete said, clearing his throat. "I know no one's exactly enforcing anything right now, but deer season… hunting… that's not usually until the winter time, isn't it?"
The men exchanged looks, but didn't appear too bothered by this thought.
"Well," Erik began. "You know how it is. Man's gotta eat. Man's gotta provide."
His friend snapped open another beer and nodded,

saying nothing.

"You know how it can get down here, Petey," Erik said, staring out into the woods and past the fire. "Remember that really bad snow storm last year?"

"Of course," Pete said. "Terrible."

What Pete didn't say was that this exact memory is why their little hunting trip right now, at this time of year, didn't sit well with him. That was in the dead of winter. It was a very humid summer and they were all sweating before a fire as a testament to the fact.

"Our town - the older folks call it a village, because that's what it says on any map you can find - our town, that winter... a lot of people went hungry that year. Three people even died. We said to ourselves, we said to each other... we wouldn't allow that to happen again. If there was game to be had, we would be out there in the woods, earning our keep."

Pete felt as if he had struck a chord, so he didn't push further and instead visibly grimaced to emphasize his sympathy. It was as if Erik could read his mind, if only for a moment.

"Yeah..." he said, over the fire. "Winter. It's not even September. But just think about it. Stand up and take a look around. You said it yourself, buddy. We're in limbo here. The government goons don't know what's going on, no one could tell you when hunting permits and all are going to come back normal-like anyway. When the parks and game control will have people answering phones at the office. All of that is silent. Right now..That's what's happening *now*... who knows what kind of unrest could come next? It's not exactly the same, but... but it's similar. It rhymes with it, with what happened that winter. Our town was hit with massive shortages and it left us with our pants down. We're going to get ahead of that whenever we are fortunate enough to see the road ahead with time to spare. That's all this is."

Pete just nodded, once more.

"Plus," Erik smiled, lowering the graveness in his voice. "If we hit anything prime, we'll share the first cut with you before we head out." Both of the hunters laughed and even Pete chuckled.

"I hear you, guys," Pete said, standing. "Just... thinking aloud, yeah? Let me... use the little boys' room."

The hunters began talking about something else and Pete no longer felt that they were speaking from that primitive portion of the mind, the one hellbent on survival or whatever the hell it was that he had accidentally tapped into talking about deer season. Pete looked towards the first vacant cabin up along the way and then turned towards the darkness of the woods. There was a brief moment of awkwardness when he realized he didn't want to step on any toes by relieving himself directly behind the cabin that would be occupied during the night. Weird thoughts to have, he laughed to himself.

Even though the night was a positive experience, up until and including that odd bit towards the end, Pete realized that now, standing in the dark by himself, he felt as if he had been holding his breath for hours. Now away from the fire and other human beings, the sweat that covered his body ran cold and he once again thought that he could see his breath in the air, if only for a second. After he was done, he turned back to the campfire and prepared to say his farewell for the evening.

"It was a good time, Peter," the man drinking the beer, Carl, said as he reappeared around the fire.
"It was," the other, Erik, agreed. "Hope we didn't worry you about that... survival talk. It was just funny that, well, earlier in the day when we were in the woods that whole ordeal came up, too. So it was as if, well, the wounds were fresh, is all."

Pete said that he understood and was glad that everything was kosher. He turned towards his cabin to turn in for the night when the hunter nursing the beer tsked him and went ah-ah-ah and Pete gulped, wondering what faux pas he had committed now.

"Feet check, Pete," he titled his beer towards the ground in front of Pete.

There was an iron bear-trap on the ground before him, just barely visible in the dark, reflecting the light of the fire about fifteen yards away. He wouldn't have been anywhere near it if he hadn't come back in this direction from relieving himself, but was still stunned that the hunters had set up such a monstrous thing this close to their living quarters. Perhaps, during a simpler time, this is exactly why park rangers and supervisory staff manned these parks.

"Can never be too safe out here," Erik said. "It's for protecting our cabins and our stuff and… and, well, and us when we sleep."
"Right," Pete nodded, stepping around the trap.
"We have more if you want to set some up around your place?" he asked as Pete walked away, but Pete just waved away the offer.

The sight of the trap had bothered him. He was upset and even angry with the men, but there wasn't much to do about it tonight.

NINE

On the surface, Pete and the hunters were on fine terms. Any potential upset tempers were cooled as each party had explained themselves, but seeing the illegal trap and ruminating on the whole affair was fostering an anger in Pete as he walked back to his cabin in the dark.

He was familiar with the snowstorm that they had gone all mountain man in recalling. He was also familiar with the village that the hunters were from. There had been a whole to-do about the looming storm and the need to evacuate. That was a rarity in Southern New Jersey, having to evacuate for a winter storm, but it's not as if they were complete strangers to the idea. Hurricane season was a righteous bitch, the people who lived here year-round were not blind to that danger. Pete had rented an apartment closer to Philly when this had all transpired. His grandfather, who moved about a decade back and lived in a sunny retirement community in Florida, had kept his ear to the ground for any information that Pete might have missed (or ignored) from the news.

Grandpa kept telling Pete that he needed to stock up on any "supplies" that he might need for a week inside that winter. He was very insistent on this matter. Pete told him that if he was hearing all of this all the way down in Florida, then he knew for a fact that this was getting blown out of proportion. But the old man just wanted to keep his family safe. Pete knew this and tried not to allow himself to show any venom in his language during the numerous late-afternoon phone calls. He could almost hear the man's voice now, seemingly so far away, if only because of the stark difference in the seasons.

"Pete, my friends down here, they're telling me how unprepared their people back home are. A lot of them don't even have TVs. They don't get the newspaper or anything. It's gonna get ugly."

Conveniently, watching the TV in the apartment, Pete watched some b-roll from the news showing State vehicles salting main roads through the pines and men in park ranger outfits attempting to speak to people at gas stations. They weren't that far from where Pete now stood, a year removed.

"If you say so, grandpa. I'll go shopping tomorrow after work," he had promised. And he did. His grandfather thanked him and went on a minor tirade about having a bad feeling about all of it. Bad dreams about the storm, like he could see it. Like he was there and Pete was in trouble.

Someone on the news, someone from the lower gut of the state, repeated Pete's thoughts on the matter. It was all a bunch of nonsense. It was an older lady wearing glasses that were probably contemporary in the early fifties. She insisted that this was all overblown and that everyone would be fine.

For Pete, it was. Philadelphia and its suburbs barely registered even four inches of snow. It fell on a Friday night, so disappointed school children did not even have the opportunity to miss any school. But for the hunters' families and communities in the south-center of the state, it was a catastrophe. Just an hour away from Pete, over two feet of snow had fallen. Powerlines had, as well. Some of his earliest lineman work had been on the less-destroyed areas, those closer to the city and the river. The real professionals and Feds were the ones who had to go into the epicenter.

He recalled the uncomfortable feelings he had on the matter, now rekindled on this night in the woods. He obviously felt bad for the people affected, the lives lost, the suffering, the damage... but he also felt odd about how defiantly sure they had all seemed to have been about their safety in spite of how glaringly incorrect they had ended up being. Pete was never particularly religious, despite being a confirmed Roman Catholic. He left the spirituality to his grandparents. Ironically, it wasn't grandpa that was the holy one, yet his words on the matter and apparent foresight were the ones that stuck with Pete so severely. Maybe it was just media-based anxiety, maybe it was just a rational progression in logical outcomes for a forecasted storm bearing down on a region that they were all familiar with. Whatever it was, there was one irrational piece of the ordeal that Pete clung to: he believed that whatever it was that his grandfather had dreamed about and felt, was real. It was the truth. It was based in reality. Pete was just the misidentified subject of the vision, because of his grandfather's love and concern for his own blood.

Pete was not part of any official, necessary clean up. Just the few downed power lines in his own backyard. He tried to avoid reading about or listening to anything about the storm in the immediate aftermath. It would be too upsetting and he'd probably get a bit too neurotic trying to connect the dots of his grandfather's warnings and the destruction that came about. But tonight, while preparing to attempt to sleep which he knew would likely be a fruitless, uncomfortable endeavor, he thought about those first days after the storm, after days of work similar to these. About a month after the ordeal, when he thought that the worst had passed, he remembered the loose construction of a headline that renewed this baseline anxiety, one involving finding a house in the pines smattered with evidence of desperate, sloppy cannibalism in the wake of the storm. What those people must have gone through, what they must have felt...

He would have a beer or two and watch the news, previously uncaring for the endless droning on. That wasn't an option anymore. He had ignored it, once, and now could feel the weight of that miscalculation. Ignorance was a liability, it was impossible and irresponsible to look away. He wasn't thinking about the box as something broadcasting out, but of himself and all the others like him, watching in. It wasn't a signal sending messages out, it was a lens for the silent, collective unconsciousness locked in and focused on a singular point, as if our sleeping minds slowly adjusted to peer into a great mirror beyond the void. What had happened with his grandfather wasn't miraculous or indicative of any proclivity of special abilities belonging to the individual man. Pete was just chilled with the thought that any one of us could distill this constant, ongoing conversation, the one generally incomprehensible to us all, and be subjected to flashes and images of whatever grim reality it bore.

In the waking world, we would only be left

trying to make sense of it, and likely failing to do so. The universe was constantly letting off its cosmic steam, bathing us in a wash of static feedback. But like trying to read braille on the underside of a red hot boiler moments from disaster, or trying to fix the alien plumbing of a star primed to supernova, we could never hope to actually make sense of it. And if we did, there would be nothing left of us to ever tell another breathing soul. Not in this world. Not in this lifetime.

Since then, as Pete drifted further away from the time of the storm, his need to be locked into some sort of signal had faded, slightly enough that it could comfortably no longer be described as a perverse addiction. Perhaps it was a guilt-ridden means of coping, although there wasn't really any guilt that he was personally responsible for. Seeing others suffering and having no means of assisting, that sort of just throws its weight onto anyone unfortunate enough to bear witness. Yes, Pete was far enough from the incident that simply going to sleep wasn't the almost-traumatic experience it had been immediately after the storm, but that did not mean he was completely healed. Thoughts concerning his grandfather and the strange pull of dreams and "bad feelings" taunted him with the ugly what-if: what if Pete, too, began seeing terrible things at night that he did not have any means of stopping during the day? He was going to experience such a cosmic strip of film whether he was willing or not.

He entered the cabin, cleaned himself off having been only partially visibly dirty from his seat around the campfire, and tidied his few belongings inside the building. Turning off the overhead light, he hit the cot and fell hard against the thin pillow. As he closed his eyes, he heard one of the hunters laugh loudly at something and the campfire pop, a dying ember of the flame no longer being fed. About an hour later, in his dreams, he was back out there, watching the men.

They had acted as if he was not there. This wasn't anything new to Peter. In dreams, similarly to his waking experience, Pete was generally just an observer. In that way that only made sense to a dreamer, he knew that this was some alternate take of the breathing world, an unseen version that had never happened. It was shortly before he had returned from relieving himself in the woods and almost stepped in the trap that he had no prior knowledge of. He didn't know if a composite version of himself would appear, but had the suspicion that there wasn't a fictional copy of him out there in the dark. This seemed to be solely about the hunters.

About the time that Pete would wander back into sight, the men stopped and looked up in the direction he had gone in reality. Instead of a confused stranger wandering back to the fire and almost breaking his ankle in a steel trap, the men reacted to that damned shrieking noise. This time, it wasn't a far off cry in the night, but permeated from all around, in thanks due to that horror-tinged logic of the unconscious thought. Pete was watching some highly-produced horror movie with state of the art surround sound support, recall. Before the panic of the nightmare really kicked in, he amused himself with the stray thought: he had to fix his pisspoor diet if this is how his body was reacting to it at night.

The men had stood. The fire had unnaturally simmered and almost died, if only for dramatic effect. One of the hunters, Carl, reached to his ankle and drew a small revolver. Though they both stared out into the woods, Erik began backing towards the cabin. Barely entering the cabin, as not to break his line of sight with where they thought this noise had been approaching from, he pulled a shotgun from off the table inside. Now fully armed and no longer laughing through their campfire soiree, Erik checked the status of his weapon and glanced at Carl.

"Go on," Erik shouted. "Get out of here!"
"What the fuck was that, Erik?" Carl muttered.
"I don't know, man," Erik said, all around the

campsite. "Fuck out of here...!"

He paced and approached a rusted garbage can that looked like an old oil drum. He kicked it with the side of his boot in hopes of scaring whatever it was away.

To Peter, it seemed to have happened all at once: he heard what sounded like a large metal switch being thrown, presumably the stage production of this nightmare. He watched the entire scene be bathed in this unhealthy red glow, as if it were in the shadow of a gigantic EXIT sign or the fixed light of a broken ambulance. In a lurching motion that turned his stomach, he was suddenly above the treetops, looking down in a skewed fish-eyed lens of the two men below. He was wearing the skin of whatever was making those bloodcurdling calls, and descended. Diving, it went for Carl's neck, and tore. The man screamed, Pete watched the panic escalate in the dying man's struggle. He clumsily punched at Pete's point of view and let off a stray round that pinged off the oil drum and into the dirt.

Erik raised the shotgun and fired at the creature and it mostly ignored the attack. As Carl fell to the ground and slumped over the log near the fire, the creature cried again and took flight. This time, it went far beyond the treetops and circled the row of cabins. Pete could see Erik below, stumbling for action, not knowing whether to assist his friend or take cover in the cabin. In the seconds of indecision, with one foot now on the porch of the cabin, the creature through which Peter watched descended. Erik turned and squared up against the shrill, furious harpy but the thing gained far too much momentum on its freefall. It shoulder-tackled the man through the doorway of the cabin and poor Erik stood no chance. He was ragdolled against walls, thrown against the now-broken ceiling fan, lengths of flesh being shred with each grasp of the creature which was making terrible noises the entire time.

The source of light in the cabin had broken the moment the second hunter was being thrown to his demise, but that red glow still permeated through the entire scene that Peter was witnessing. Once the creature was done with Erik, it dropped the body on the front of the porch and effortlessly tore off into the night, leaving Pete behind in this nightmare, alone with the two dead hunters, a dead campfire, and a sea of neon red. Even with the creature whose eyes he had watched through was now gone, he still felt as if he were being watched. By something else, but something similar enough to the winged and clawed beast to instill a permanent unease. Pete approached the man on the porch. Erik laid with his neck broken and unmoving face looking up towards the stars. The blood that pooled around him expanded out, and started dripping into the dirt. Against the constant red light, his blood could have been any liquid, even water. It was the horrified look on the dead man's mangled face that gave away the grim reality of its nature.

Pete did not know how long he looked at the pooling blood, but was broken away when something disturbed its surface. Although it was the middle of summer, snow had begun to fall over the pines. He stood, looking around for whatever heralded the next act in this macabre performance, but nothing came. Now firmly off in the distance, he heard the call of the creature once again, but it was no longer furious or foreboding. It almost sounded like it was gloating. He sat down on the porch, not too far away from the body. He did not know what he could do, but felt that if he did not make too much of a commotion, he would remain safe from the same fate of his neighbors. Sitting in the shadow, he felt the glow begin to feel physically warm, the red light growing bolder.

For a moment he had thought that the nightmare was over. He blinked and was again laying in his own cabin, in the cot, but that red light still washed over everything. Pete screwed up his eyes and rubbed at them, now very much over the whole ordeal and no longer wishing to dwell within the nightmare. The red remained, and he realized he was not alone. The front door of his cabin was open, and a figure stood just beyond. He immediately sat up in bed and prepared to fight off whatever or whoever it was, still very much swimming in the wake of the horrific murder. But the shape didn't have talons or wings or that telltale screech. It, instead, spoke. Very slowly and very low, as if it was far away and on an old radio signal moments away from breaking.

"You cannot stop this from happening," it said. Stupidly, Pete sat in silence, then answered.
"Carl and Erik?"
"No. All of it."

The red light's intensity began to grow, white overpowering the red warmth. It felt like that fuse was, in fact, going to fail, and end whatever this interaction was. He realized that that snow was gaining intensity, as well. It blew into his cabin on an unfelt breeze.

"Wait," Pete said and stood.

He ran towards the open door and the figure beyond. Immediately, he ran face-first into the closed door of his cabin. Recoiling from shock, he looked around. It was mid-morning and nothing in his cabin was disturbed. The door was just simply there. Closed. As if he had woken up from a terrible dream, which he realized and hoped beyond hope was exactly what had happened. He could still smell the smoke of the campfire from the night before on himself and coating the grounds outside.

There was nothing in the world that would have stopped him from assuming the worst. He thought of his grandfather and his bad feelings about looming storms. Pete could only believe that once he opened the door to his cabin and took a few steps towards the neighboring cabins, he would find the massacre that he had watched last night in his sleep. He did not want to open the door, but he likewise could not stand here forever in his underwear. He moved towards it.

TEN

Of course, everything was just fine.

The sun never really shined directly on the semicircle of cabins, but the rays that did bleed through the taller pines momentarily disoriented Peter as he looked through the mist. Not ten steps from his porch did he realize the absurdity of the expectations he had been building for himself, standing there behind the closed door. The still smoldering fire was calm, the few cans of beer crushed in a perimeter of the sitting logs were not dashed in blood or visera, and the door to the hunters' cabin was closed. When he was about fifty yards away, he weighed the necessity of physically knocking on the door himself and ensuring that they were unharmed. Hungover, perhaps, but not mutilated. He realized both that he could ignore this idea and that he was still wearing his underwear when he saw Carl come from behind the building himself, having presumably relieved himself in the woods.

"Uh," he stopped in his tracks and chuckled at Pete's

appearance. "Morning, Pete."

"Oh, damn," Pete said, clutching a robe he wasn't wearing for additional coverage.

"I didn't..." Carl was giggling like a child. "I didn't think you drank *that* much last night, buddy."

He pointed Pete up and down.

"But I've been there!" he laughed again.

"I'm sorry!" Pete stammered, then owned up. It was a bit funny. "I... thought I saw a deer or something and wanted to see what it was up to."

"A deer, eh?" Carl said. "I thought we definitely scared any of them away from home base by now. But hey, if one of our secret goodies snags one, maybe we'll have a repeat barbecue tonight, right? You like venison?"

Pete was not, and wouldn't be in a million lifetimes, prepared for this conversation at this time of day. He waved off Carl's small talk and turned to get ready for work. He could hear the man still chuckling to himself as Pete made his retreat.

Well, he had thought to himself. They're not butchered. That's... that's good.

Although it could ultimately be rounded up and described as nothing more than a bad dream after drinking some cheap beer and being out in the somehow dehydrating humidity with his hunter pals, and consuming a ton of heavy food before sleep in the process, Pete didn't know how he could be expected to just clean up a bit, get dressed, and go to work as if nothing had happened. He did not linger too long on the thought, but considered how absurdly unfair it was that our own restless unconsciousness could subject us to a night of nigh-trauma, the six or seven hours being inorganically expanded into an experienced bout of psychological torment, and then just expect us to wipe the slate clean the next day.

We weren't the survivors of some terrible criminal on the prowl or some stranded refugees at the mercy of a natural disaster, just someone trying to get some sleep – and you could only hope to convey your experienced pain to others as what was, ultimately, just a bad dream. Why was it that our dreams could recklessly deal so much damage with one night of suffering, while never even possibly being able an attempt to do the opposite, to heal, in the same amount of time? Even the pretty dreams could only hurt, by painting the rest of the waking world dreary in comparison.

But that was what he was expected to do, to move on, so he did.

The condition checking of the trail had become second nature to him by this point, but it was honestly just pleasant enough to get out there and have a change of pace from his little false neighborhood in the pines. Of course, the similar landscape of the utility route would cause Pete to stop in place and listen, or scan the deep treelines every so often, but he had not felt any looming danger on this morning's walk. He was in good enough spirits that he even tuned into the professor's show on the handheld, just to enjoy the grating sound of a familiar voice. Or rather, voices. It was the AM crew, guest-hosted by students at Stockton College. Pete wondered if Maggie knew them at all... or if she had yet received his photo in the mail. He smiled gently. The sun was warming the dew on the exposed grass and sand of the Pine Barrens and the air was crisp. It was a pleasant morning after so much mental anguish the night before.

-she clearly acts as some sort of protector of the Kirkwood-Cohansey, Roger, the girl's voice said.
The what-now? he asked.
The aquifer that our state sits on, that's under the Pine Barrens, she said.
And that's... good, right? he replied.
Well, the aquifer isn't good or bad... it's certainly good for us, I mean. It's our life force, so to speak. I'm sure older cultures regarded it as highly as we are ignorant of its importance. But believe it or not, our state has done a decent job of preserving it.
Ooh! Kind of like them telling the airport investors to shove it, back in the fifties, he said.
That's right. Exactly. The jetport expansion would

have been horrendous for everything ecological. For listeners who don't know, the powers that be decided that we need yet another major airport in the region. And they parceled out land in the Pine Barrens for the endeavor. Obviously that never came to pass, she said.
Well, not yet, at least, he said.
Always so optimistic with you, huh…

Pete amused himself by wondering if these two would be the most interesting people to talk to on campus, or social pariahs. There was not a lot of venom in the idea. He thought about how he felt being seen by others when he was actually with Maggie and realized that that was exactly how he felt next to her, in comparison: a pariah. It wasn't anything she did. He loved her, of course. He just felt… perhaps inadequate was the word.

For another hour he listened to the two prattle on, talking about folklore, the Loch Ness Monster, and other creatures around the world that were supposed protectors of whatever region they inhabited. Pete was sympathetic to the idea. He liked it. Thought it gave some credibility for the creatures existing in the first place. In a roundabout way, it gave us all a reason for existing. There was some existential disappointment tinged throughout it all, of course. Why did his species (apparently) have to be such a blight on the planet that potentially magic beings had to spawn to keep us away and in some cases punish us? He thought about every piece of litter he let slip from his hand since he was in grade school and chided himself for his selfishness, no matter how petty it seemed as the day went on.

In the peculiar way that the professor's radio programming always managed to, he thought about how potentially applicable it was to his own life and the adventures of this young summer. Perhaps the nightmare he had the night before was a projection of his own distaste for the hunters' behavior and their rowdiness. That guilt he felt for trashing a bag of fast food out on the interstate, perhaps the violence of whatever monster he was in his dreams was their comeuppance, however dramatically overkill and violent it might have been. How much of the content he was listening to was merely himself looking into a mirror and coping by relaying his own experiences onto it? Pete knew he was lonely and was eager to relate to anything he could, even if it was silly monsters and UFO stories on the radio by voices that he found acted as surrogate friends during his day job. It's not as if he was a social butterfly when he was off the clock. Good ole' Mr. Z would probably laugh at these thoughts, caught up in his own ways like he was. It was a sobering, disheartening thought, but for a moment Pete realized that the grumpy old man was likely the closest thing to a friend he had right now. He definitely pushed that thought out and tried to continue listening to the show as he walked along the route in the woods.

He had successfully compartmentalized portions of the dreams that he thought could only do damage to dwell on. No one needed those visions of violence and gore. It wasn't like the movies he liked watching as a kid. It felt too real. So he thought about the powers in play. What was the creature that he watched kill the hunters? Who did he feel was watching him when he was himself once again, on the porch, staring at the massacred body? And finally, who was the silhouetted figure standing on his porch, moments away from what he thought was confrontation, which turned out to be him sleepwalking himself awake? Pete rationalized that there were three unique entities in the dreams. Besides, you know, the dead hunters. But they were okay in reality, so it was alright to consider them extraneous in the context of this absurd line of thought.

The context of the morning's program did strike something in him. You always heard those old stories, about things in the woods lashing out at those it thought were either a threat or just plain disrespectful. Spirits. Or something else, something more feral, something with claws and maybe wings. In some ways, Pete could empathize with its disdain for the hunters, even having reminded himself that it was just his own thoughts encouraging the nightmare. While he appreciated not being totally alone in the woods for however long he was on this job, he did feel that his camaraderie with these fellows was potentially running thin. They had cleared the air, but there were obviously some things that they could not see eye to eye on. What the hell was all that about the snowstorm? Sure, feel bad for your hometown, he got it. But they were obviously young-ish and resourceful enough. Take care of your own without making the world a sundered battlefield in the process, yeah?

Pete had walked this morning's length of the trail by noon and was already on his way back when he reached the spillways. He had been cognizant of the recent bouts of rain, but it had not seemed nearly dire enough to explain what he saw. The creek that usually trickled along the pebbled, muddy floor was swollen with recent runoff and looked like a miniature river. The flow was not heavy and did not appear dangerous, but to see the natural creek lapping up on the manmade concrete partitions was a surprise to Pete's tired eyes. What would flooding in the Pines even look like? A few country highways blocked off for days at a time until the floodwaters receded? He took out his laminated map and checked off the site of this curiosity. Might be a good question for Mr. Z, whenever it was the next chance he spoke to the man.

It was enough to warrant curiosity, but not necessarily concern. This time of year, forest fires were common. Sometimes, when wetter seasons permitted, controlled burns were rolled out by the State and local governments. The Native Americans were known to do this, as well. There was a cycle involved, one very dependent on this controlled rebirth, the ash, and the sandy soil. Pete had no idea what the exact details were or the intricacies involved, but assumed that with everything else tied to bureaucratic red tape, any current burns would also be at a standstill. If there weren't controlled fires going on, it stood to reason that natural, uncontrolled fires could crop up in their stead. If nearly-natural running water was currently at a surplus, as told by spillways he now observed, well, that seemed like a good thing to him.

The pines were healthy enough that they would not burn to the ground spontaneously.

ELEVEN

Early on in the assignment, Pete was prone to losing some time out on the trail. He would easily cover miles, not realizing he should have stopped and had lunch on a few occasions. Whatever was happening today was different. He felt as if he was starving and his usually reliable sense of direction was utterly failing him.

Pete knew that he was never more than a few miles from a country highway in any direction so long as he stayed on the path. Harking back to his brief stint as a Boy Scout, he ensured that he never strayed off the trail. After noon had come and gone and he felt as if he was somehow going in circles on a completely linear route, he began to wonder if he was not sick with something. Maybe even poisoned. Certainly inching towards dehydration.

When he felt as if he had begun lapping his route, with certain landmarks in the forest appearing familiar for the tenth time today, he tried to assess where exactly he was on the trail when things began repeating themselves. Perhaps there was a detour he was not previously aware of, a sub-path that circled back to cut the miles-long trail into an accessible, shorter walk for casual hikers. The only thing was, he reminded himself, that his team and other employees of Mr. Z's crew were the ones who cut this trail. He even helped to mark it out, for Christ's sake. He was the rookie of the group, sure, but even he would have noticed that at some point. The laminated map he now clutched like a religious talisman was useless.

Either way, he knew he had passed the fire watch tower about an hour ago. If he was still stuck in whatever loop he had found himself in, he would soon be approaching it once again, from the opposite direction. Clouds had begun to form in the sky, but he was not afraid of any precipitation. At this point, some rain might be refreshing. Whether it was due to an oncoming storm or the increasingly frantic motions of his person, he didn't know, but Pete realized that almost all ambient noise and signs of wildlife had completely diminished. He began to think about stories his grandpa had told him when he was younger. He felt stupid to be creeped out by them, but he was thinking of fairyfolk and children disappearing when he managed to distract himself from the harmful nostalgia and saw the roof of the firewatch tower through the trees.

Okay, we're at Apple Pie HIll. This is a known landmark. I'm not far from the Carranza Memorial and the road. Pete stopped and looked around in every direction. Besides the tower a few hundred feet away, he couldn't discern any other way off the portion of the trail he was on. Frustration was mounting. He looked at the disappointing map once more and stuffed it into his jacket. This was nonsense. He was getting off the trail now and getting some god damn lunch.

After practicing the prayer of the insane and repeating the loop another handful of times with no resulting change in an outcome, he was ready to scream. It was even beginning to get dark out, the sun having begun its descent about an hour prior. Once again standing in the line of sight of the tower, he grumbled and climbed through the knee-high scrubs and weeds that separated it and the trail. Salting the wound, when he entered the clearing of the fire watch, the gentle rain that had been falling began picking up in intensity and the wind chilled him. Up above, there was a single light on the exterior of the tower's cabin.There was no one around and the weather was getting shitty. He would try and talk his way out of anyone upset with him for trespassing. Hell, if anyone was up there, maybe he'd be able to call for help.

The rusted iron staircase to the tower

strained under every step. Pete didn't know how safe it was, but was thankful that there were at least stairs and not a single, precarious ladder or other method of ascending the structure. He would have likely talked himself to standing out in the cold underneath the thing had that been the case. Reaching the top of the stairs, he looked out. The flat of the Pine Barrens extended in every direction. Even in the best of conditions, he knew that he wouldn't be able to see any massive cities or landmarks with the naked eye. The dots of Atlantic City and Philadelphia could only taunt at this distance. Out here, you were kind of in the middle of nowhere. Like he had previously told himself, he could see the major road through the Pine Barrens, sloping in either direction about a half a mile away. The hunger pains and exhaustion prickled up like a rash at this sight, the knowledge of rationality confirming what he knew to be true. What was existentially frustrating was that he could easily see the road from up here, but if he went back down, he knew he would somehow never reach it on foot. Something was wrong.

Instead of fighting it, he would try to breathe and see it through. Even with the uncomfortable night and morning he had, he knew that things had been going alright recently. He would force himself to go with the flow, be malleable and accepting of whatever unknown was at play here, instead of stiff and at the whim of breaking against an uncaring universe.

At the far end of either side of the horizon, he could see the pale glow of civilization beyond the bar. He knew he could reach someone eventually and return. He turned to the cabin of the tower and peered through the dirty glass. Pete was shocked to see that it looked… comfortable.

The door was unlocked. He then tested the lightswitch. The exterior bulb flipped on and off with his gesture. There was a single wooden table against one wall with a heavy block of radio equipment bolted on. A microphone and pair of headphones were left next to it. There was an empty stove in one corner of the cabin, a simple cot in the other, and a pair of boots under cobwebs opposite the radio equipment. A structural pillar stood in the center of the room. For a moment, all of Pete's professional ambitions faded away and he felt at ease with the idea of becoming some sort of ranger on behalf of the local fire departments and wanted to spend his days out here, watching for the trickle then billowing towers of smoke coming from the dry, sandy pines, and calling the trouble in to any fire department that would listen.

The fear of meddling fairy folk rose up again when Pete chuckled to himself and realized just how randomly comfortable this did all seem.

Lightning dashed across the open expanse of the sky and he realized that he was stuck here for the immediate future as it was. If he was the victim of some trap in folklore, so be it. Not much else he could do about it now. He clapped off the detritus of his brush-stomp in the corner near the cobwebs and removed his boots. No longer a chuckle, but a full laugh erupted from the solitary young man when he sat on the cot and realized there was a box of hiking provisions against the wall. He ate a stranger's trail mix and thought about how he would eventually pay the original owner back.

Getting settled in a bit, he removed his jacket and realized he had not been listening to his handheld radio throughout the concerning portion of his ordeal. His eyes wandered to the radio equipment in the corner and the single red light that showed that it had power and was in standby mode. Before getting too comfortable, he walked over to the desk and tried to turn the thing on. Of course, it was tuned into the professor's radio station. It was running a syndicated weather report that, on top of all of the nonsense Pete had dealt with in the last twenty four hours, made his stomach sink.

There was a hurricane warning. Though it concerned Pete and made him think about the past snowstorm and the hunters back at the cabin, the broadcaster, either from Philadelphia or Atlantic

City, discussed the pending storm as occurring over the weekend. In the extended explanation of the hurricane warning (versus a storm watch), the terminology drifted in conjecture and ebbed, saying, "tomorrow's storm," or referencing, "tomorrow night." The days tended to run together in this job, as Pete was learning, but he knew that the night spent talking with the hunters was no later in the week than a Wednesday night. He would have guessed it was a Monday, given a chance. The timeline of his walking the utility route this morning, of seeing the flooding spillways and getting lost on the trail, no longer synced up with his own sense of time. There was no way he was potentially harboring a few days of missing time. But the voice on the radio told him otherwise.

Before stumbling back to the cot, Pete engaged the lock on the door. He knew he would hear anyone climbing the structure, the rusted stairwell of the fire watch probably older than himself by a few decades, but he suddenly felt particularly vulnerable. He was desperately counting out days on his hands and straining his eyes shut trying to make sense of it. Days of the week. Lost time. The distant, numbed taste of sickness and a parched tongue. Was anyone concerned about him? Mr. Z or the hunters, did they even know anything was out of line? Did they even know he had been gone? Could they help even if they had wanted to?

On the radio, the professor's voice broke in after the weather report, the too-much-cheeriness that occasionally irritated Pete was like a strong salve on a wound. Jarring, but god damn what a relief.

Out in the darkness, lightning flashed. Before the reliable roll of thunder could sound, Pete started. He had thought he had heard the single retort of a gunshot. He was once again thinking of the hunters who might as well have been a continent away, although he knew, in reality, that they were no more than a few miles removed in these same, endless pines. He moved and checked the lock on the door once again, no matter how futile a gesture it might be. He kept trying to remind himself that he wasn't in any real danger. Nothing had been chasing him through the woods, he had never felt such a threat. It was only his exhaustion and dehydration messing with his brain's chemistry. He insisted on it.

Pete laid down on the cot. If he had the luxury of just settling in comfortably, he would face the wall and try to sleep. Instead, he faced the door and could not help but stare at the frame. Every now and again, the lightning storm would flash the terrible shape, the shadows blocked out and remaining as an afterimage even when he blinked and tried to lie himself to sleep. He could swear that he saw the shape of that strange man from the campsite, previously only known and seen when bathed in the red, inorganic light of his nightmare, standing out on the platform of the tower. The only relief was that the figure's silhouette was no longer there when he shut his eyes and tried to force the image away. The lightning would overexpose the rest of the cabin and its windows on his eyelids. They did not do the same to that which was not there.

Given the situation he was in, Pete was stunned that he felt as if he could physically afford sleep, just drift off in this strange room fixed above the trees. He would not argue with the respite, successfully blocking out the multitude of issues and variable considerations that seemed to gather around him, standing in the shadows of this momentary lapse of anxiety. The situation was strange, but if physical exhaustion was great enough to override those preconceived instincts geared towards self-preservation, it was likely that he had lost more time out there on the trail today than he previously considered.

TWELVE

The landscape of the dreams had returned, painted in the palette of a nightmare. Of course it had.

When the vivid dreams struck him back at the cabin, for a majority of the experience there was never the explicit threat of danger. He was its perpetuator, Pete had seen whatever had dealt that violence, or at least had the power to. But he was no longer wearing the skin of a creature with the ability to fly or the claws to rend flesh. He was a spectator being shown these images for an express purpose, though he couldn't discern exactly what that was. Maybe it was just his body punishing him for allowing it to be placed in such a predicament in the first place. A handful of granola and a single bottle of water had been his only refreshment for days, apparently. His grandfather with his scouting upbringing and military experience wouldn't be mad, just disappointed, an infinitely more striking blow.

If the red light from the sky designated the silhouette of the man he had previously seen in his dreams, the oversaturated and over-contrasted film he now watched behind the lens of sleep was trying to fill him in on the events of this world he had stumbled upon on behalf of another entity, because though Pete was local to these lands all of his life, he had ebbed towards the city and then later, the country roads. Never the endless pines. He was ignorant of its soil and something from beyond refused to tolerate this blindness. Perhaps it, whatever *it* was, was only disgusted and sought to educate. It knew Pete as innocently ignorant. His void of knowledge was not intentional or done in malice. As the dream unfurled before him, he was distantly aware that if this had ever changed, he would face bodily and mortal harm. And now that he was seeing behind the veil, however briefly, ignorance would no longer merit a sufficient excuse.

The fear that was held at an arm's length tried to rationalize what he was seeing as merely topical and brought on by his physical exhaustion. He was tired and there was a storm coming. He had discussed the last major storm that had happened in the region with the only other people he had spoken to in the last month. Although they were separated by seasons, the severity of the storms were comparable and as such, appropriate to haunt his resting hours. A hurricane was bearing down on the southern portion of New Jersey. A blink ago, it was the blizzard in which one small town in the Pine Barrens faced extraordinary suffering. That nameless village, one that was only barely on most modern maps, was now where Pete's avatar stood.

Like a black and white film strip, he saw the approach into town. The road that he had been diverted from was not too far from here, much closer than he had realized when the story was relayed to him secondhand from Carl and Erik. He had to remember that he was never that far away from the campgrounds or their place of apparent tragedy at all times. Never more than a few miles. Suffering like that doesn't just soak into the ground and disappear. Perhaps the snow that suffocated and concealed all that had transpired had merely been cycled back into the perpetual system of this earth and was now coming back in the form of the storm that had begun dripping down heavily in pelts on Pete's shelter in the sky as he slept.

The snow was relentless. Most of the buildings in town appeared ready to be torn down long before the storm, Pete surmised, but he knew that people were living in them. Well, there were people in them. "Living" was being generous. Some structures showed modern amenities. As he drifted through the storm, unencumbered by the driving snow, he was aware that most of the village's inhabitants were either passed out drunk or panicking over the care of any children they were responsible for. For some, it wasn't an emergency, not yet. Many of the villagers were hardy, decent people, and this was just Mother Nature doing what she did. Some of them, however, as it was in any community, were reckless and arrogant against what they faced. Those who fell into this group might not have even known what they were yet dealing with. Perhaps they were just a few drinks in at this point, considering this as an additional excuse to get blitzed and not worry about any other duties for another stretch of twelve hours. Pete's attention was drawn to a dark figure at the far end of town, emerging from the woods.

It was not the specter from his cabin's porch or any sort of supernatural deity, it was just a man, as the realest monsters typically are. Somehow, without a single word uttered or any additional context provided, Pete linked this stranger to the two men he had recently met, the hunters Erik and Carl. This man was inadequately dressed for the snow and seemed to be struggling with the provisions he had in hand and was desperately trying to get home. Even with his skin exposed to the cold, he was drenched in sweat, strung out on something that Pete couldn't determine if he had another twenty years of living under his belt. The man knew only that he had to get home and that he could enjoy the crate of booze he clutched to himself under an arm like a running back. Time skipped and the man had reached his house, an unremarkable rancher with a shattered front porch light. He had begun yelling at an older lady and child inside almost immediately. Shouting escalated throughout the hour and staccato bursts punctuated the unnecessary violence.

Pete's vision stood in the snow for a few lingering moments before jumping ahead another twelve hours. It was still snowing at daybreak. Skip. It was a week later and silent.

There was over four feet of snow and a thick layer of ice coated on top. It had stopped falling a few days ago, but no one had come to or left the house since the man had gotten home during the storm. How the snow had drifted and then later frozen, Pete realized that there was the slightest pronouncement from the front door of the house, a failed struggle to simply get out. The drifts had buffeted every visible window and he doubted that there was a roof hatch or any sort of special mechanism installed on the simple structure. When he watched the man stumble home, barely coherent, he had apparently entered into a tomb of his own making. There wasn't stopping what he was about to see, though he knew he wanted to pull away. The vision was drifting towards the house over the shelf of snow and ice and he knew he was going to see something terrible.

There was the man, sitting on the center of a sagging couch, looking as if he had nodded off. Upon closer inspection, his head was draped backwards from the apparent explosion of a single gunshot through the mouth, an obvious suicide. What drove him to this point was made apparent by the subsequent drifting through the ruined house. Blood was everywhere, perhaps left in the wake of his tumultuous arrival. Things were broken and glass was shattered everywhere. Unresolved domestic issues brought on by the natural disaster and the altered state of the man who stumbled in from the storm were the culprits. The older woman was dead in the kitchen. Pete knew this and tried to look away, but this only steered him towards a child's messy bedroom where a small figure was hidden under a nest of blankets and gore. It was horrible, but somehow seemed a softer end than that which the rest of the house received.

Almost immediately, the vision tore back to the kitchen and Pete could see the deranged series of thoughts that had led to the man's demise, the one who killed himself on the couch. A fight had happened and had continued to escalate. He hurt the woman and then the child and then was trapped with what he had done. He had tried to leave, multiple times, but the house and the storm wouldn't let him. Damage was concentrated on the woman's thigh and the greased-over stove in the kitchen was left open, the stove-top also still hot. The rabid animal of a man had considered and attempted cannibalism after ending whatever semblance of a family had existed in that house, after a week of being forced to see and smell what he had done. The trauma of it all felt palpable and sat in Pete's throat. He was briefly taken back to the last seconds of the man's life, the single shot ringing out and making his skin crawl and suddenly the house was empty. It was now just the grisly scene, but no longer holding the tremendous weight of the evil that had transpired. With the gunshot he heard in his sleep and the story told, it all had been sucked up and out of the chimney, to be scattered over the pines.

For only a moment, he wore the skin of the flying creature from his previous vision. It sat on the roof of the very shelter he now dwelled in, the fire watch tower. He could see the blackness of the evil erupt out of the chimney and over the pines into the sky, like a horde of mutated and mottled locusts, cast to the wind and then reforming into a tangible mass. The creature watching this cocked its head and Pete could feel its brow furrow. There were two entities with great power now cohabitating the Pine Barrens and the one that sat on the roof was particularly territorial. Pete knew that only by the power it had displayed. It let out that inhuman screech and took off to investigate the intruding force. The police, or curious neighbor, or wildlife that first discovered the murder scene then knocked against the door of the house and Pete was taken back to the living room with a dead man. The knock sounded again and he bolted awake. Hail fell heavily on the roof and windows of the fire watch.

Lightning glowed in the distance and he was comfortable, but moved by the scenes he was now trying to process. Something had shown him that for a reason. Whether he could act on such information he didn't know, but could appreciate the knowledge in some far off, primal corner of his still-sleepy mind. Even if it could only serve as a warning. It did not seem like something that a shovel or crowbar or park ranger could assist with. Maybe the only winning move was to get as far away as possible and let it sort itself out. At the thought, thunder rumbled and he remembered the peculiar position he had put himself in. He couldn't leave. At least not yet.

He stood and moved towards the radio on the desk. He sat down and turned it on, if only to pass the time. There was no way for him to know what time it was to begin with and he was still too groggy to get his bearings. Pete considered this his seasonal adjustment of that winter in the apartment, or his days just weeks ago in the hotel, turning on the television late at night, just to feel something resembling being connected to the breathing world. What were we if not a series of bad habits and toxic patterns constantly shifting ever-slightly, to accommodate the progress of time? It seemed to Pete that you broke those cycles by either shaping up and maybe having a kid and giving them a better go at things than you had, or dying. Poor Pete never gave enough thought to the matter to consider that those aren't always the silver bullet solutions and instead only create a compounding effect, each of them in different ways.

Pete was competent around hardware and machinery, but had never really had the opportunity to screw around with high-end radio equipment like the "station" he found before him. It wasn't anything extensive, certainly not anything like the actual station that Professor Emerson worked in... thinking of the goofy old man and the college kids made him feel less lonely. He screwed up his eyes in the dark and twisted the knob that most closely resembled the console in his car and, to a lesser extent, the portable radio he kept. He didn't want to make any potentially approaching strangers (or creatures...) even more stealthy by shutting out the real world, but without much thought, he put on the puffy, oversized headphones that were draped across the desk and listened, his gaze going through the dirty firewatch windows and the storm still brewing outside, over the dark, endless pines.

Evening, night owls… or rather, good morning, almost, the familiar voice of the Professor came through the headphones. *Hope you're staying dry out there, the Powers That Be claim that the hurricane will make landfall by noon. So much for passing the coast through the night, haha!*

However pleasant it was to hear the man, Pete blinked thoughtlessly as he tried to process this information. He had completely abandoned any preparation for the coming storm in his galavant through the woods… his little trip and lost hours of time had cornered him up in the sky.

Of course, that means you only get more young Joel Emerson! That is, until the National Guard comes and takes me away or we get flooded out. We'll see! Anyone who has seen the station knows it's like Fort Knox, we're probably much safer here than anywhere else they'd want me to hole up!

Pete knew that this wasn't true.

Either way, I'm going to run a few minutes of our commercial sponsors (and tidy up around the station if I'm being honest), but if anyone else is riding out the early onset of this storm with me at this late hour, perhaps I'll field a few callers. Recall our topics this week: corruption in Atlantic City, paranormal geographic guardians, evidence of life after death, and orbs caught on film! Let's get to it!

As the tinny jingle of a local car dealership came over the signal, Pete thought that he might have underestimated the old man and this pet project radio station of his that was apparently making his retirement quite enjoyable. Whether or not it was a profitable endeavor, who knew, but here he was, long after midnight and still cheerful as ever. Pete was a quarter of his age and at least twice as miserable. He felt the slightest bit of guilt at the silent, momentary quips he had dealt the man. The only consolation was that he was never outwardly rude to the man. A few more commercials played and Pete inspected the large box that made up most of the radio equipment, one button was marked with a piece of electrical tape. Next to it was one painted red with the word EMERGENCY painted in white. He glanced back at the less alarming one. In the dark, it looked like the word CHIRP was hastily written on the tape with permanent marker. Pete clicked it twice.

For a second he was dizzy, but he realized this was because the sound of the radio station had doubled. He was reminded of the time he and Maggie had tried to win concert tickets from the rock station and he briefly heard himself twice, in person and through the radio, before he answered some trivia incorrectly and was disconnected. It was the Professor, talking to him.

"Uh, Apple Pie?" he asked.

"Apple Pie?" Pete repeated.

"Well… maybe the storm's got things acting crazy. My friend, it says you're broadcasting from the Apple Pie Hill fire watch tower, is that correct?"

Pete blinked then cleared his throat and sat up. Duh.

"Oh my goodness," he shook his head. "Yes, sir. Professor, this is the firewatch. It's Pete Demetri."

It was the Professor's turn to blink through a response, but he was even quicker than Pete had been.

"My boy," he laughed. "What the heck are you doing at the tower?"

"It's a… long story, I guess. But," he thought through a delicate lie that was mostly the truth. "I'm working on utility lines out here like we discussed. Got lost and I took shelter from the rain."

"Good thinking, Peter," the Professor said. "Might want to head out before the wind gets too crazy though."

As if on cue, the glass in one of the tower's windows

panes strained against the whining gale outside.

"Right," he said.

"You know, we're actually not too far away. I'm not sure how far your lodgings are, but on a clear night, you can see our signal tower if you look real hard to your… to your left, I believe."

"God," Pete muttered. He could see a small blinking red light about a mile away. How he had missed that, when literally everything else was the dark shadow of the pines was beyond him. "I would wave, but I don't think you could see me, huh."

"No, Peter, I don't think so," and they both laughed.

"Say, Pete… why don't I put you on. We can discuss some silly goblins or whatever tickles your fancy as it relates to my show. You should head out within a few hours, but if you're awake anyway, why not pass the time?"

He thought for a moment. He didn't even expect to get in touch with someone else on this radio, let alone Joel Emerson, but here he was. Laughing, even.

We're back, night folks. And I have a local legend, Peter Demetri, lineman of the Pines himself, holed up in a fire watch tower, protecting all of us as we sleep, ha!

Pete wanted to refute this claim, something that wasn't exactly like but felt like stolen valor, but he let it slide. He used the show's weekly topics in review as his blueprint to help guide himself along the Professor's ramblings. He never used to really be into the paranormal stuff, but having listened to the show throughout his day job's many excursions out into the field, he realized how much he had soaked up through verbal osmosis. They had discussed UFO sightings over water reservoirs in their humble New Jersey, over the river crossing up at Lambertville, and off the point at Sandy Hook Marina way up north. These were interesting, but Pete explained that he never had a personal encounter with a flying saucer, so they weren't super personal to him.

Ever the expert radio host, the Professor probed this point.

Well, Pete, if you've never seen a flying saucer, what have you seen?

Pete thought this over and though he couldn't explain it to himself later why he had done it, it certainly felt right to. He removed key locations and actual names, but he recounted his last couple of nights in the Pine Barrens, about the hunters, about his dreams and their story about the blizzard, and most importantly, about the things he saw in his dreams, the strange creatures that seemed to be at odds with one another. Somehow, the man on his porch, always bathed in a glowing red light, never materialized in the equation. Perhaps Pete felt as if his message was still only meant for him, however selfish and confusing that may be.

That's quite a story, Pete... the Professor said, for the first and only time sounding genuinely alarmed. For a moment, Pete was worried that he had finally gone off the deep end and told a story too bizarre even for his loony shock jock. These fears were abated. *You know how highly I think of you and I think it's remarkable that some strange guidance out in the world apparently feels the same way! The moment you find safety, try to meditate on these experiences. I've always said that we are on the precipice of a great awakening, of love and knowledge and loads of hokey other feel-good nonsense. We need younger people like you to be our stalwarts in whatever the new age beckons!*

They both laughed, but Pete genuinely appreciated the sentiment and the strange ravings of this man who had been a stranger only a few weeks ago.

Alright, Pete, well, we'll let you go and try to get back to your homebase. Dawn should be breaking within the hour. Try not to get between those two... entities that have been invading your dreams, deal? Don't get in a fight between your two older sisters when Mother Nature is running errands, right?

Pete nodded and lowered the volume on his end. "Yeah..."

THIRTEEN

With the daylight breaking through the swirling storm, the way home was easy, but wet. Approaching the ring of cabins, Pete saw no sign of the hunters besides their usual detritus outside. If they were sleeping or hunting, he had no clue. He was stopped in his tracks, however, when he noticed a strange car that slowly came into focus as he rounded towards his shack. There was a pale blue Pinto station wagon and a slight figure on the porch.

"Maggie?"
She turned and leapt at Pete, smothering him in a hug.
"Peter! Local legend!"
"W-what?" he asked, confused and choked.
"Nothing's going on on campus. I'm on summer term, but classes are canceled because of..." Maggie gestured all around, referencing the looming hurricane. "Everything going on. My roommates went home for the term and I got bored watching TV so I turned on the radio and... well, you probably get it. I called the station as soon as you hung up. I

talked to that Emerson and we extrapolated."
"Why were you up so late?" Pete laughed.
"You know how I am, Peter," Maggie said.

And he did. But this pleasant surprise turned a bit sour when he became cognizant of their situation.

"Well, I should probably get the truck somewhere safer than… the middle of the woods."
"Come to Stockton with me. The dorms are all safe and they have the gymnasium set up in case things get really bad. They're all safety-certified and whatnot. Say, isn't that what you do?"
Pete realized how little Maggie knew about his actual professional ambitions and although it hurt a moment, there was a second of endearing sincerity in the statement.
"In a way, I guess. But sure, campus is a good idea. Mr. Z will kill me if I sink his truck in a bog or something."
"Is Mr. Z Italian?" she asked.
"Yes. Terminally. Why?" Pete said.
"He sounds like my grandpa," she smiled.

Pete followed Maggie's light blue car on the rural highway through the Pines. His truck wasn't even that big, but he sat at two whole heights above her as he trailed her at a comfortable pace. The storm hadn't even yet fully arrived and the trenches on the side of the road were flooding. The sandy soil had congealed to a murky mess of mud, pine needles, and dirt and the pygmy pines looked like terrified, blighted creatures emerging from the depths, pleading for mercy. The taller, endless pines beyond were indifferent.

Though it was the early hours of the day, it felt as if the sun was already setting. Road flares and a blinking traffic blockade made Maggie and Pete slow to a stop. An army truck was parked behind the blockade. Up ahead, the road was already being swallowed by the floodwaters. Just barely. A soldier, likely from the nearby base, waved and smiled as he approached Maggie's car. They exchanged a few words and then Maggie's reverse lights lit up and she backed up to turn around. When she was facing Pete up in his truck, they both rolled down their windows and blinked through the rain.

"They're closing the roads. The reservoir to the south of the road is flooded. They're concerned about the northern one now. The dam and pump system is still active, but they're worried with the worst still to come. We can get to Stockton no problem but have to head back and turn off about two miles back. Then it's a forty minute shot to the school. The man said they would permit the truck to pass, but not my Bennie," Maggie said, referencing her car. "It's not safe."
"Alright, then let's-" Pete nodded and then was struck by the realization. "Oh shit."

"What?"

"The professor."

"Oh, no…" she said. "Is he going to get stuck there? He probably drives a shitty little-"

"He does. I've been to the station. Hell, it might be one of those Pintos they actually recalled," he pointed to her station wagon that was presumably not prone to spontaneous combustion.

"Well, there's no way we have time to drive all the way back, drop my car off, go get him…"

"Don't worry about it. What if we… what if we park your car at Apple Pie Hill and then all pile into my truck. It'll probably get hit with… sticks and whatnot, but it's not going to get carried away by floodwaters on top of the hill. We'll stash it, get the professor, then get to safety."

Maggie gripped her steering wheel for a moment then agreed. He asked if she knew how to get there and nodded. It was one of the only landmarks out this way, as it was. They began rolling up their windows and she caught Pete's eye to blow him a kiss as she drove off. He waited a moment for her to safely start away and took a breath to assess the situation. He thought that leaving the fairytale world of his night at the fire watch would be a gentle descent back into normalcy, but here they were, playing out like a sappy side-plot in an action-adventure movie they rented from the video store. At least Maggie was here, that was a nice surprise.

But there was a whole season of nighttime trauma to meditate on, per the Professor's orders, and the whole natural disaster unfolding before them.

Alright, Pete thought to himself, time to get going. He nodded at the soldier that was still standing in the rain, turned the truck around, and started back.

FOURTEEN

Now that the plan had been formed and the dreamlike state of the morning seemed to drip away with the warming (however still adequately wet) weather, Pete thought about the peculiar series of events that had led to him being all the way out here in the Pine Barrens during hurricane season. In the years that he spent closer to Philadelphia, "hurricane season" was always just an acceptance to expect some thunderstorms and hear about damage from down south. It was a far away specter, akin to the tornados of the midwest or blizzards in the mountains. New Jersey had its bad weather, but was geographically diverse enough to force these blights into minor hiccups in normalcy, not a recurring natural disaster.

The lowlands of the region made sense to him as being susceptible to flooding, but with just how much pineland there was, it never seemed to be a major cause of alarm. People weren't densely packed. It wasn't like a city block being under water. He wondered how much preparation on behalf of the local military bases and locals themselves had gone on over the years, undetected to his ignorant, outsider perspective. He supposed he was getting a first hand lesson. The conceptualizing of this "lesson" almost made Pete slam on the truck's brakes. Lesson. Training. Experience. The entire utility project's portfolio was in the damned cabin. All of the excitement that had transpired had completely blotted out his entire reason for being here in the first place.

The truck slowed on the county highway. No one else was around, and why would there be? They were comfortably at home, hunkering down, or already miles away. He thought about what the soldier had told Maggie. The truck was hardy enough to get through the early stages of lowland flooding. Hell, if the idea was to get both of them to the Professor and then to safety, a brief detour to the cabin wouldn't hinder any of those plans. In fact, it might be a critical means of testing its reliability. If he couldn't get to the cabin, he would get Maggie and retire to the safety of the open road, to carry them towards campus or wherever, just away from this area that was already flooding. The fact that they would be driving *towards* the coast where the storm was making landfall was one that was not obvious in its inherent danger to them. Not yet. All useless details. Once they were all together and once they were all on campus, they would be alright. That was the company line. He turned off towards the cabins, the roads already messier than they had been only an hour prior. The truck was, thus far, as reliable as ever.

The hunters' cabin was still dark. Standing water was now accumulating outside of their porch. The truck dug through the muddy path that made up the small village's road and Pete arrived at his own cabin without any fanfare. He stomped his boots twice on the deck and fumbled for his keys. He stopped and looked up, realizing that the door had been left open, only slightly, and imperceptibly from the truck. Had he not locked up the night before? He didn't give his traditional "hello?" before entering a strange place. Pete was in a hurry.

As the door slowly swung open, pushed by Pete's boot, the ceiling fan wasn't turning and no lights had been left on. All that had greeted him was the static buzzing of the refrigerator and the damp smell of the air turning stale. He turned to grab the binder on the table when a floorboard creaked behind him, from the corner between the bed and window that had its shade pulled all the way down, almost to the floor, a space that bore no light from the outside world. He flinched, but did not turn. He simply composed himself, one hand kept on the binder.

"Who are you?" Pete closed his eyes and asked. He knew it wasn't either of the hunters. He knew it wasn't an animal, but he wasn't sure it was even a man. It was certainly the shadow that had been standing on his porch that one night and a presence that had observed most of his time at the tower. Its voice betrayed any humanity it may have previously feigned. It sounded far away, as if through an old, failing walkie-talkie. In any usual setting, Pete might strain his ears to hear more clearly, regarding the source of the sound as if it had fallen deeply into a drainage tunnel and Pete was the last chance of reaching in, too far into the too dark, to retrieve the forgotten device. But here, in the confined one-room cabin, with his back to the figure, the voice was directly against his ears, simultaneously everywhere and miles away.

"I'm just a visitor," it said.

"What do you want?" Pete asked.

"I wish to preserve a few small things dear to me."

"Are you going to hurt me?"

"I have no interest in doing so."

"Then why stalk me. Why show me terrible things?"

"That is not my doing. Those things... draw my attention, as well," it whispered.

"Can you stop what's going to happen to the hunters?"

"Stop?" the voice paused. "I don't think anything can. They are caught between two greater beings, beings that must settle their affairs on their own.

But… if you must know, the hunters, their end will be humane. They shall be drowned. Not… as the images imply."

Pete wanted to turn around and shout at the shape, angrily, but he could not move. He could only continue this conversation that had removed any haste he may have carried.

"People are going to die, and you won't do anything to-"

"I told you, Peter Demetri. That is not my doing. You've seen through the eyes of that which wishes to rend flesh. You see what is borne of rotten flesh. It was of greed, it is greedy, it grew arrogant and earned the ire of something else of this land. Now, she has returned and her charge is perceived to be in danger. She's fulfilling her duty and acting like it's… like what you may call an immune system. 'Everybody wins,' is the saying, isn't it?"

At this, both the wind and rain picked up in their intensity outside. Pete knew that if it was darker outside and in the cabin, a dim, red glow would be pulsing off of the shape in the corner.

"You said you wanted to save something… what is it?" Pete asked.

"It is stored somewhere in the building that speaks to the sky," it answered, simply.

"The radio station?"

"Perhaps," it was in no rush, despite the apparent

urgency of everything else in the world.

"Perhaps!" Pete muttered, almost laughing. "For Christ's sake, give a straight answer-"

"As it stands, the caretaker of the building will perish in the same waters that are currently smothering the hunters' village and that which will overtake them in the woods. Their fates are sealed. The waters will continue to rise through the end of this week. What I seek at the radio station will survive. Its keeper may still live."

"The professor?"

The voice didn't answer.

"And you cannot intervene?"

"I did not say that."

"I wish I had a gun right now."

"I do not see how that would help your situation."

"It probably wouldn't, but I'd probably feel a lot better," Pete smirked as he pictured turning on heel and shooting the stupid cardboard cutout of a noir detective that he pictured in his mind.

"Your people's military are actively deciding whether or not to abandon the systems on the southern reservoir. They believe it is a lost cause. If they do, the building you speak of will be lost entirely, including its host. If you can convince them to keep the systems engaged, he may have a chance yet. But time is running out."

Pete suddenly felt relieved of the conversation. He picked up the binder and moved to the door.

He turned towards the corner which seemed artificially darkened. The figure was still there.

"Alright then," he said, looking towards the floor. "Thanks, then…"
"We may yet meet again, Peter," the voice seemed to fizzle away. "Things forgotten are not irrevocably lost." Pete knew that if he turned on the overhead light, he would be alone in the cabin. He stepped off the porch and was driving the truck away from the cabin within seconds. It was the last time that the row of cabins would have a human visitor for over a year.

FIFTEEN

The routes between the campsite and the utility trail and the fire watch and the radio station and every variation of the lot had begun to develop burn marks in Pete's subconscious. Like the bleeding scar across his increasingly tattered laminated map, he was beginning to see the shape of these drives behind closed eyes, dug in deep in the mud of his mind. In a prettier circumstance, he could probably have amused Maggie with having her drive the truck as Pete gave the directions to any of the noted landmarks while he sat in the passenger seat, blindfolded. Maybe they could laugh over that sort of ordeal once they got through this storm, assuming that the locations all survived in a solid-enough state. Pete did not know how enthused he would be to suggest such a game if, heavens forbid, the radio station was destroyed in the floodwaters. That is not even considering the human life that was possibly at stake...

The flooding in the trenches on either side of the road was already swelling up and covering portions of the blacktop pavement. It had sat like pooled rainwater, as it always had after any amount of rain, when the day had first started, but now Pete could see the early-on movement of water gaining volume and strength. Like some unseen force drawing the standing water to the largest flowing body of water nearby, whether it was the stream in the spillways, a creek, or a river, or hell, even the ocean, the floodwaters were rising and developing a mind of its own. He was both thankful that Maggie was nearby and that they were abandoning her low-riding, unwieldy station wagon with the conditions outside worsening.

The ghost of a smile faded as Pete sat with these thoughts. Sure, she was here and had obviously cared enough to follow a voice she heard on the radio long after midnight, and they'd enjoy some bizarre week locked up with one another and her classmates and away from the storm, but there were critical steps that first had to take place, here and now. Did the work truck have the fortitude to conduct what was essentially a rescue mission? For that matter, did Pete? The voice of the shape in the cabin came back to him as he made the second to last turn off before he would (hopefully) be within eyeshot of Maggie and the tower. The battle plan he had been silently developing was contingent on the words of some... hallucination? Ghost? Alien? Perhaps he needed to heed the Professor's advice even more direly than he had previously imagined.

He didn't need to simply "meditate" on these thoughts, he needed to work through something. Clearly. It was one thing to have dreams, but to throw yourself and a loved one into the eye of a looming storm nearly at the recommendation of something you think or feel you saw... he steeled himself and thought that there would be time for a little light self-hatred after they were safe.

He could bolster himself as much as he could in the truck's cab, silent sans the windshield wipers and pattering rain outside, but his stomach sank immediately upon seeing Maggie standing under the fire watch tower, too cheerful in the storm, her station wagon and windbreaker and hair and smile too bright against the gray and green drab of the sodden, endless pines that stretched for miles in every direction. That they were on the hill that held the fire watch tower, the highest elevation in this sub-continent of lowlands, only made the pines' infinite sprawl that much more apparent. But there she was. And now he had to tell her about his change in plans. He could see her smile drop, only slightly, when he pulled up towards her, but then rolled down the window instead of angling the truck to invite her to step up and in. Pete was not intending on staying long or taking her with him, not yet.

"Mags," he said, awkwardly blinking through the

rain.

"Should I get in, Pete?" she asked, confused.

"Not yet. You'll be safe here. Did you park Bennie?" Pete asked, clumsily. Where else would the station wagon be?

Maggie nodded and pointed to a small divot in the hillside, a protective canopy sheltering the vehicle. She moved past the distracting small talk.

"Pete, what's going on, I thought the idea was, 'pile into the truck and get the Professor,' and then we'd go straight to shelter?"

"We will... we will, but we have time for that... we don't have time... here," he thought through the words as he said them, trying to convey his plan and not confuse either of them by accidentally oversharing where this information came from. "Maggie, I need you to go up to the tower for me."

She involuntarily pointed at the structure above and behind her.

"The tower? In a hurricane?"

"It'll be safe until late tonight, at the earliest, trust me," Pete said. He knew this, because the shape in the cabin knew this. Somehow.

"And how the hell do you know this?" she was starting to get upset.

"Don't mind that. There's a radio up there. I need you to 'chirp' the emergency signal, it will probably connect you to a paramedic squad, or fire department, but with things like they are, maybe even the military dudes driving around."

She was still confused, but Pete's referencing of seeking outside help by the trained, uniformed professionals seemed to calm her down a bit.

"'Chirp' the radio..." she repeated, her head tilting just slightly.

"You can't miss it. You'll do fine, I know it," Pete said, nodding his head, trying to get her off to safety. "Tell them, 'keep the systems engaged on the southern reservoir, do not abandon the equipment,' something like that. They'll understand. They have to."

"How would you know anything about that?" she asked, sincerely.

"Why do you think I'm working out here in the first place?" he decided to lie. No one besides Mr. Z really knew what it was he was doing out here, anyway. He'd appreciate the gag.

"Oh," Maggie nodded. "Right. What are you going to do?"

"I'm going to get the Professor, right?" he patted the steering wheel.

"Alright," she said. "Be careful. I love you."

"I love you, too," he said.

Pete watched as she turned and slowly climbed the slick metal stairs that wrapped around the fire watch until she was out of sight. He was confident that he could get down to the radio station without an issue. It was just a matter of the Professor cooperating and what the conditions were as they left. It shouldn't take them that long, right?

As he made his way towards the station, he became aware of two things: the rain was only getting stronger as the day went on and that the radio station itself seemed to be positioned at the bottom of a bowl-shape trench gently dug into the earth. The quarter-mile approach of the paved driveway diverting off of the main road highlighted the latter. Before the truck had even picked up speed, Pete could feel the vehicle sliding across the slick path that ended up in the parking lot of the poorly maintained building.

In all of the excitement of the morning, he had failed to ever tune into the station's programming. Had he done so, he would have experienced the peculiar double-hearing that he had recalled the night before communicating with the Professor directly over the fire watch's own radio for the second time in as many evenings. The dizziness of the consideration drifted into reality and Pete clutched the steering wheel. It may have been an optical illusion of sorts, it may have been some sort of pavement treatment that did not respond well to the torrential rainstorm it was not used to being subjected to, or maybe Pete's nerves were finally getting the better of him, but one way or another, as the truck descended the path and towards the parking lot, its driver lost control of the vehicle and ended up driving through the glass doors and lobby of the building. Pete would have been able to hear the crash through the Professor's ramblings at only a half-second delay from what he was traumatically experiencing in real time.

The accident itself wasn't that bad, just horrendously embarrassing. The reality of the storm overwhelmed any financial concerns Pete had. He knew insurance or some sort of deus ex pecunia would swoop in and salvage the damage. He was here on a mission. The sound of easy listening vibrated through the station as the Professor himself came stumbling out of an office, very clearly having heard the crash and gone to an emergency musical break. He saw the white work truck resting against the front desk with mud, broken glass, and branches strewn about the lobby, the rain now flapping into the open space, as well.

"Peter?" he asked, genuinely concerned.
"Hey there, Professor," he said, meekly. "I'm here to-" but he was cut off, as it was at that point that the truck's airbag finally detonated and knocked Pete out cold.

In the hours that had passed since Pete's accident, the Professor halfheartedly attempted to board up the broken doors and stop the teeming floodwaters from breaching the lobby. Somehow, he had succeeded, partially due to the surplus of sandbags he had been stocking for the very occasion. But due to how the building was situated in the bowl-shape dip of the lowlands, the parking lot outside was under a foot of water, the small spans of space outside of the lobby doors now the last remaining shoring before the deluge. When Pete blinked awake, he did not know if it was almost night time (not enough time had really passed) or if the weather outside was simply smothering all available light.

The thoughtlessness that the old man displayed upon his awakening at first irritated Pete. The man didn't seem all that concerned that his radio station was slowly being submerged by rising floodwaters or that someone had just driven through the lobby door. Pete calmed himself by considering that the old fool might be going through something like shock. He felt sympathetic and even slightly envious of the prospect. This was no longer a lighthearted rescue mission, but something dire for the both of them.

What Maggie had done or had failed to do, Pete couldn't know. The fact that so much time had already passed and the floodwaters were still rising led him to believe either she had failed to use the radio properly, she was ignored, or that all of the above had actually worked, but their continual usage of the reservoir's pump systems still failed due to the severity of the hurricane. You can do everything right and still fail. You can take all the precautions in the world and still drown. Perhaps it was this realization that made the always-too-cheerful Professor the silent, solemn figure Pete now followed around the office.

Pete had asked the Professor if there was a second floor and he only shook his head. He was trying to resign himself to their fates, even if it killed him to speak for the younger man's life on his behalf. Pete did not yet accept this. He asked if there was roof access or even an attic. At this, the Professor looked up.

"You know what… if this is the end," Pete ignored that part and listened to the man. "Let me at least show you some very special things before we go. At least, let me be around some of my favorite things."

It turns out that there was an attic towards the back half of the radio station's office building. Once Pete followed a shivering Joel Emerson up the pulldown ladder, he felt that the term "crawlspace" more adequately suited the room they had climbed into, but that was neither here nor there.

Beyond the typical refuse found in office environments (boxes of supplies long past expiration, cleaning tools, old pieces of mismatched hardware, and the like), there was an oddly organized corner of the cramped space. The dirt that coated most of the surfaces was absent in this one corner of the room. The iron shelves were cleaned around the objects that they stored and glass or plastic cases adorned some of the items up there. It was almost like a cut-out of a miniature museum, hidden away up here in the attic. Between the dusty area of the attic and this museum space, Pete noticed some army surplus rations, a wrapped canvas sack, and a rolled sleeping bag and wondered how often and how long ago had the Professor been so absorbed in his work that this area may have served as a studio living space of sorts. The peculiar old man seemed to be composed infinitely of surprises.

As Pete squinted in the low light, the Professor drew out an electronic lantern and turned it towards the items. Pete marveled at the collection. There were photographs of various members of the armed services from present day going all the way back to colonial times. There was a piece of silverware that had apparently been on the Titanic. There was a hat belonging to a man who Pete had never heard of, one named H.H. Holmes. There were postcards from all over the world, as well as university memorabilia, such as pennant flags or buttons. There was a piece of scrap metal toe-tagged "Silver Bridge" and various other pieces of construction supplies from around the world, presumably from wreckages. Pete stopped when he saw a framed portrait of a well-dressed military man, two scientists, and an alien right out of one of his silly midnight movies. He looked at the Professor and laughed. They would have a lot to discuss if they made it out of there.

It was just a pure collection of the bizarre, pictures of things that looked like Bigfoot but weren't, old newspaper clippings about the Jersey Devil itself (herself?) and other weird animals that had shown up in the region. All of this was very heartwarming and Pete wondered if the Professor had ever shown these items to that production club of students he had helping run the station. He felt privileged to be up here, either way, and it was an incredible distraction from the overwhelming thought that they were both about to die. Pete realized that Professor was first resigning himself to losing the station and all of his work, which was an understandable pity. But once the severity of the flood picked up, that was when he had made peace with his apparent demise, surrounded by odds and ends and a stranger turned friend.

From behind them came a slight buzzing and then Pete noticed the familiar red glow that had been the hallmark of so many recent nights. There wasn't any hesitation this time. He turned on his heel and was prepared to argue with the shape from the cabin.

"Oh, what the hell do you want now!" he said, furious. But almost immediately, Pete's anger dropped and he smiled as he finally looked the entity in its eyes, the unspoken made clear.

EPILOGUE

There's no telling what Maggie would have done if she had been able to see the truck's collision from her vantage point. The distance and weather were too much. Even on a clear day, the brush would have obscured her view. She had taken Pete's instructions to heart and climbed the tower, finding the radio console exactly as he had described. There ended up being time to kill.

The urgency of the ordeal slowly wound down. Maggie pushed every thought inching towards disaster away. If Pete had failed, there wasn't anything she could do to help him immediately without also dying in the process. The outside of the fire watch's booth was like the inside of a car wash, heavy buckets from the sky slapping against the straining glass. Somehow, the cabin remained comfortable. The first hour of her time there had been ignoring the outside world and attempting to reach someone through the radio itself.

The "chirp" function and the "emergency" button did what they were programmed to do and she eventually got in touch with both a rescue squad and a dispatcher close to the military base. There were a series of painfully slow relays and irritating repetitions of what Pete had told her, and though there was no telling if they actually understood what she was asking of them, the message was delivered. She had done her best and now she had to wait for either the others to come back in the truck and then, together, they could all reach shelter, or for her own rescue, now courtesy of the friends she had made over the airways.

Then, hours passed.

The rain would continue, but in one relatively calm period, she peeked from outside the cabin over the canopy and saw that the hill itself was now almost like an island. There was a muddy current running around its base. She could only assume that the main road was completely impassable and that Peter and the Professor had been forced to stay at the radio station. If it was possible to see the station from the tower, she had no idea. There were no lights visible in the rain and she could not discern any of its rooftop equipment through the storm and above the trees. Somehow though, it wasn't an entirely unpleasant ordeal. She knew it might have been some sort of survival mechanism, or maybe she was physically unwell and colder than she thought she was because of the soaked nature of her surroundings, but she wasn't all that scared. It felt as if there was something pleasant in the air, even through the hurricane currently bearing down on the coast. At this point, the eye of the storm was about two states south, still over the ocean.

Night would soon be falling. Even accounting for the hurricane that would soon be in the region, it would somehow be a more peaceful night than the one that had preceded it, if only after one last piece of business. The shape that had been speaking to Peter through dreams and at his cabin had told him the truth about the hunters. Whatever it was that had been conjured by their fellow villager's greatest sin wanted them dead. Maybe they were blood relatives. Whatever it was that had sought their necks had also trespassed on these endless pines. An unspoken agreement had transpired and a compromise had been met. Last night, as the hunters fled the tent they had pitched in the woods, a cacophony of screams and screeches had erupted in their minds. As they ran from the torn tent and from each other, each of them saw their own nightmare version of the world beyond.

One instantly stepped into one of their own bear traps and experienced what he thought were swarms of dark, black insects erupting from the ground, reaching any orifice they could. The other had made it about a half a mile before seeing, somehow, ground water seep up from the sandy soil of the pines and chase after him. For a moment, he thought he was some by-product of the looming hurricane, but then he was also accosted from above, by black, reaching claws, he knew he was out of his element and that this was a mortal reckoning, not merely inclement weather. With the demise of the hunters, somehow the world felt softer, no longer anticipating the storm, but ready to experience it.

It had been dark when Maggie woke up from resting on the same cot Pete had sat on. At first she thought that emergency vehicles had finally reached the tower. Maybe some sort of amphibious vehicle, or heavy-duty rescue truck had arrived. Emerging from the cabin of the fire watch and looking in the direction of the radio station, she saw that she had been mistaken. Like the sun breaking through black clouds over a beach, a single ray of brilliant light shone down from the night sky. It was as if a searchlight from the stars had focused heavily and singularly on the property of the radio station and held it there for a few moments, before blinking rapidly and ceasing.

Maggie turned around, as if to see if there were, bizarrely, any other bystanders to have witnessed the light from the sky. Of course, she was alone. She would remain as such for the rest of the night.

With daybreak, the waters had already begun receding. The hurricane ended up not making a direct landfall and shot off from the shore once it had reached Atlantic City. There was minimal damage to the boardwalks of the shore and inland flooding, but those who were used to these seasonal storms considered this one of the lucky, calm ones. A truck did end up coming to the tower to help out the stranded young woman. It was a part of the local emergency response, neither a military vehicle or ambulance. Just a pickup truck with the name of the municipality painted on its doors.

The reality of the last twenty four hours fell on Maggie's shoulders and she insisted that they get to the radio station and help the others. The two strangers who were in the truck eagerly obliged. One of them said, "that's what we're out here for, isn't it?"

The station had seen better days. Sitting at the bottom of its divot, a foot of standing water still flooded the entire property. The truck pulled up to the edge of the spontaneous pond and the three passengers disembarked, Maggie immediately trudging through the water and calling out Pete's name. There, she discovered the bizarre scene of the truck somehow ending up within the lobby of the station, the sandbags that had gone up behind it, trapping it inside, and all the refuse and contents of the office floating around, as if they were tiny, non-sentient prisoners having escaped their holds.

The entire building must have flooded, Maggie thought. There wasn't a high water mark present because it seemed the entire thing had been submerged. She was worried about live wires and the like for a moment, but desperately needed to confirm whether or not they were still here. High-stepping through the flooded building, she reached the end of a hall, she saw a drop-down attic door built into the ceiling. Climbing up, she beat a fist against the floor as she discovered that it, too, was empty. She told the men from the truck the situation. They all had assumed the worst.

The men expected her to be inconsolable, but she maintained that airy, almost aloof, cheerfulness that had come over her during the storm. While this may have looked like a tragic loss and accident during the hurricane, she knew it would work out. Once the rest of the flooding had receded, she had revisited the fire watch every night that week, waiting to see that light over the pines, once again. Sadly, it did not immediately come.

She visited every night. As life began to become normal again, and that much more demanding, she came once a week. Then, once a month. The grim considerations had begun to grow: was she just blocking something traumatic out? Was this being naive? Pushing these thoughts down, Maggie told herself that, fine, maybe that was the case. Then this drive out to the woods was just her form of therapy until she could really meditate on what had happened. It was over a year before she saw the light from the sky again.

The blue station wagon labored up the incline to the fire watch at Apple Pie Hill. The silly Polaroid photograph that Pete took and mailed her was still sitting on the passenger seat with a handful of books in a canvas bag. There had not been any indicator that this night would be any different than the others. She really thought something might occur on the night that marked the exact year of the disappearances, but that would have been too convenient. It came and went without commotion. A week later, she was back on her usual schedule. So, she decided to make the most of the pleasant summer evening, climb the stairs, and watch out over the endless pines.

Eventually, the red beam returned. Maggie had almost killed herself flying back down the metal stairs and as she peeled out in the clumsy vehicle, towards the former site of the radio station that had been forced into a hiatus.

Approaching the dark building, her stomach sank. It was exactly as it had been on all those previous visits: dusty, dried mud everywhere still from the storm, windows broken out, siding falling off. But still, she killed the engine and stepped out of the vehicle. There was movement inside of the lobby. There were voices. There was laughter. The Professor and Pete came out, almost arm in arm, but more so like kids who had just had the day of their lives at a carnival. It would be revealed that they had no idea how much time had lapsed. To them, it could have been the very same night of the storm. You never know how very worried the people who love you are until you come down from an exhilarating high.

Maggie did not know whether to slap or to strangle him, so she instead leapt and hugged Pete. The Professor chuckled and turned around, finally seeing the full condition of his radio station.

"What the hell..." he muttered, as a few things must have dawned on him.

Pete and Maggie looked at one another, still embracing. For a moment, he thought about Mr. Z and what a confusing ordeal this must all have been on his end. His mind was racing, but he couldn't form the words. They would come with time. They would have to. He did, in fact, have quite a story to tell.

www.ingramcontent.com/pod-product-compliance
Lightning Source LLC
Chambersburg PA
CBHW061534120726
48001CB00004B/1545